Green Grass, Hidden Water

Green Grass, Hidden Water

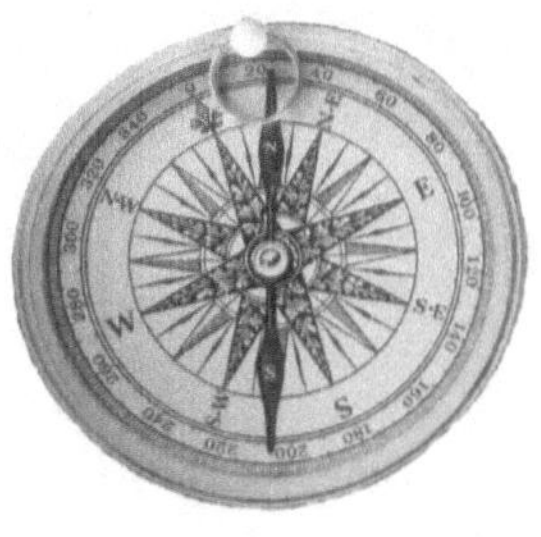

Jack Esposito
2020

ISBN: 978-0-578-63596-5

Interior drawings and paintings by Donna and Jack Esposito
Book Design: Carolyn Vaughan, cvaughandesigns.com

Printed in the U.S.A.

To my wife, Donna and our three children who always inspired and encouraged me to keep on writing. Special thanks to my book designer and mentor, Carolyn Vaughan for her technical skills and endless support. As well, to all who seek to bring about peace and journey with heart.

Contents

Green Grass
Hidden Water

In the end it was as if a vivid dream had occupied my conscious mind. The years ensued and were glued to a task, a goal of unrelenting (crushing) command (pressure). It enabled and salved my vision without interfering with its pristine purpose. It was a force that motivated behavior, a font of strength promoting vigor.

This childhood awareness motivated and merged with a young man's enthusiasm and the older, more seasoned man's experience. Fantasy, play and astonishing certitude were constant co-travelers as I forged a pathway into existence. This effortless flow prompted lofty self-images which nourished growth and partnerships of varied types: the athletic, academic, romantic and other ties along the way. The Himalayas and desert valleys of the mind, heart and at all times, the soul, marked my ups/downs in every pursuit. I tasted the grand and the sad.

There were detours, of course. The dream, it seems, embraced the "many roads to Rome" theme. A central diversion was the call to perfection, which was spawned by desire and a narcissistic proclivity to always be right. To do the right thing in the right way in everything became mantra. The payoff was immediate. What inexplicable pleasure to know that one is better than everyone else, no matter when or whatever the situation. The model of masculinity with testosterone pulsing and unmatched sex appeal ever-ready for engagement. My journey was a hodge-podge of do's and don'ts without any maybes or perhaps.

The challenge to be perfect in word, thought, act and the ramble of emotion was formidable. Always guiding, prohibiting and enticing, this mantra was a constant companion. It drove me onto and into many diverse involvements. The Christos, religion, and salvation tallied several years of conscious engagement, flight and continuous affirmation of this quest for perfection.

A visit to Los Angeles demonstrated this fixation on perfection. Following a separation from a woman who loved me, I headed west. The trip proved exciting and most productive. Several sales-based commission jobs delivered money, women and the endless amenities. Jill, who worked with Bob Barker on the TV show "The Price Is Right" showed me more than what was behind all those curtains. Her slender legs, ample bosom and well-formed buttocks provided hidden fortunes in those beneath-cover eager encounters.

There were other single night episodes laced by narcotics and alcohol. The upside of a downward spiral. But, in the moment and for that moment, I was perfect. My style and LA were in sync. A perfect fit. All dots were connected as were beats of the drum which kept pace.

There was haze and some shade; however, most days were sun-filled, sea shell shined. The glitz and glare were amazingly unfair because few people let down their tents. A defensive promenade barred these fickle people from being genuinely present to others.

Siliconed, plasticized bodies were the call of the day. Some women had more chemicals in them than the local industrial plant's daily produce of these concoctions. And safe sex had yet to become a household word, nor part of the grade school curriculum.

Within six months, boredom grabbed hold and a longing for home and sanctuary from the tinseled beautiful people took root. My work as an auto sales person, tour guide, and periodic waiter in a posh restaurant was smothering me. The next day came and went as did the next and the next. The following nexts were nothing more than mere marks on a calendar. I became indifferent to time and frequently to place. Life was work, eat, sleep with periodic play. At times it deposited a dull, tasteless something in my mouth. The type of blandness we avoid at every turn in life regardless of mood or level of enjoyment. More often than not, this unexciting attack on taste buds was accompanied by rote behavior patterns. The same old that only became older. My clouded mind and weakened heart prompted me to return home. Los Angeles had proven to be an unremarkable episode in my life. Trudge, trudge, trudge.

It had been a gallant escape filled with delight. On a walk along the beach while the ocean brooded into the night, I fell asleep on a large rock near a fishing pier. As dawn flexed its way into the new day, I realized what had taken place. My stroll was so relaxing that I floated, feather-like into a child-like sleep. The whisper of waves had not detoured my path to the world of dreams. It was a pleasant moment. This moment reminded me of a similar experience. I remembered my early days in Newark. After the end of a semester at Rutgers University, I would go into Manhattan and ride the subway rails to Brooklyn and beyond. During these mini journeys I became lost in thought about who I was becoming as a young man. Many a night I had fallen asleep while swaying back and forth on the rails only to be awakened by the loudspeakers call alerting "end of the line." I was ready to return home.

I drove back to Pennsylvania in record time. Route 15 North into Utah to 70 East through San Rafael Valley and onto Colorado soil across White River National Forest and across the Rockies. Denver seemed to appear in a flash, then onto 76 North to route 80 East at satisfied speed and periodic roadside rest stops for short naps. Gas stops and food time were also respites from the grueling monotony of myopic stare. It was 65 to 70 through 80 miles per hour and the continuous purr of my Saab 96. It was a two stroke, cylinder engine with a modified gear shift on the steering column. What a wonder to experience this amazing machine step through its paces. Gas mileage was excellent since cargo included a duffle of clothes and several bottles of Mexican Tequila.

I enjoyed the tantalizing taste of tequila during this episode of the perfect trek within the dream. Two or three T finger shots with lemon/lime and a dash of salt helped the medicine go down. As did T with orange juice to witness the rising sun and capital T in the majestic Marguerite to help keep me on track.

The trudge through Nebraska and Iowa left little for the imagination 'cept the open range and endless sky. The splendor of Tequila and memories of good times and some serious hangovers provided ongoing entertainment for the mind. To be sane is good or, at the very least, the illusion of such is most attractive.

Chicago, Cleveland and two great lakes seemed to whiz by. Soon, the unfettered beauty of western Pennsylvania timber—a well-kept secret—filled my senses and refueled my source. I was close to home of course. Pittsburg was the place. The confluence of rivers, steel mills and soot. The turf of Pirates, Steelers, Duquesne and Pitt Universities. The legendary Carnegie and the red stuff of Heinz. Penguins marked this soil as well.

I grew up in New Jersey, the hustle-crazed, mad driver, factory infested city of Newark. The underachiever to New York City and insecure contributor to the 'American Dream' scheme. But more of this later.

Perfect was a full-time preoccupation of my energy and focus. No respite here!

It consumed my conscious day and fueled my subconscious nights. There was, in fact, no flight. I was a victim of diligence and devotion to a cause. This compulsion-like urge to be without flaw or limit became my center, my destiny. There were no squiggles, nor sways. My drive was unequivocal and persistent.

This incessant drive was evident in my pursuit of work. I was to be an educator, the opener of doors and creator of new vistas. A guide through the hoops and an encourager of free, independent and responsible thinking. My choice was psychology with a focus to keep one's feet in the real world.

Freud was studied but not embraced; Jung spoke to me and provided image, language and vision to my evolving craft. Serendipity and synchronicity brought friends and acquaintances. Women were not exempt from the magnetic-cognitive-positive, connection. I sought, felt and promoted change, directly, unexpectedly and certainly without plot or plan. How seemingly easy these came about while not looking or pre-meditative structuring.

My life appeared perfect in a somewhat imperfect way. Perhaps this was the illusion. An ongoing companion called mirage. A life filled with outstanding accomplishment, increased pleasure and money galore. 'La Dolce Vita' indeed! Or so it seemed.

I became entangled in the contesting schools of method: Carl Rogers and B.F. Skinner. The focus centered on person-centered insight and behavior modification. To guide a personal insight into one's life via creating new pathways to remediation of personal problems or utilizing reward for desired behavior with acknowledgement and physical payoff. It was not an either-or tangle. The experience centered primarily on the question "do we choose" to do what we do because it is the right thing to do, or do we comply with expectations in order to receive rewards. Put another way, "what psychology/psychologist would I want to be president of the world?" Maslow, Allport and existing thought helped me arrive at an answer. To choose on the basis of insight and understanding is where I took my stand.

My courses were well attended and enjoyed by a broad spectrum of students. Some were serious, others adrift in the shifting cultural winds. Most were uncertain about future plans and life mission. All in all, the best course was "Personality Theories" followed by "Individual Differences" and "The Absurd Mind." Each course overlapped the other, somewhat, but maintained an independent approach to the wonders of Psychology.

The opportunity to delve into the theory, practice and evolution of psychology was both fascinating and most useful on the personal level. My purpose in the classroom followed the same orientation. Students liked my open, friendly presence and management of class. I used a facilitative rather than an info-centered lecture. The large discussion group frequently hovered over the topic/issue of relationship and commitment.

Many wanted open-ended relationships without enduring commitment. Others favored the conventional pattern. My occasional re-directing of these discussions targeted individual differences amidst massive collective orientations. The epi-center focused on how to maintain good standing in a group yet be a complete individual geared to personal choice and orientation. Autonomy, freedom and responsible behavior loomed large.

THE BLOSSOM

It was a seasonal rain. The uncertainty of early summer storms and the rumble-tumble roar of thunder, and the splash of lightening led to awe and pensive wonder. It was impossible to ignore the storm's majesty. Power cloud formation and an abundance of dark hues of deep grey, blue, and at times, black. Multi-colored clouds with sprinkler holes accompanied along with the wind and whip-like crackle.

Jennifer, a graduate student at the U and I had just wrapped up a date. Our relationship began as mentor and student but quickly moved into the sexual relationship category. Driving away from her apartment, my intent was to return to my place and get some sleep. Rain tattooed the windshield as the vehicle effortlessly found its way into the mountains. I kept one window cracked a little in order to assist the struggling defroster with the challenge of the encroaching foggy dew. This onslaught was extremely heavy at times and negated wiper activity. Nevertheless, fatigue and limited vision pressed my attention to its task.

As I drove, my thoughts returned to Jennifer. Her unrelenting attractiveness was like a magnet to me. I could not be close to her without wanting to merge our bodies. She was eight years younger and a most engaging lover. Slender bodied and athletic, Jen knew and encouraged active participation in the Kama Sutra positions. Her ongoing invites to "just try it" told much of her past and obviously, her early youth. She was most efficient at her tutoring. Time with her was always fun filled and good times.

Tonight, however, was a sex free evening. A restaurant near her home is where we shared an early dinner of fish and a garden salad mated with a bottle of Merlot. We kissed tenderly with a prolonged embrace followed by a penetrating eye contact and brief laughter. The laugh reminded me of the way young children laugh at the end of a play period. We closed out the night with a hug. Were I more settled, I could easily and willingly have married Jen. But my life had much dust to settle.

The next morning, following a quick cup of coffee and crackers with jelly, I marched out to the back yard to do some lawn work. I preferred a 4.5 gas engine Poulan that proved easy to push over 100 by 100-foot open range. Tree and bush trimming were also on the agenda.

Halfway through the lawn cutting the phone rang. Jen responded with an anxious and hurried voice. Could I go hiking with her along the Monongahela? A lunch had already been packed as well as a bottle of my favorite wine. H2O included. It was a beautiful summer morning. Not too hot or humid with a pleasant, refreshing breeze. A day for outdoor activity. Oh well, tomorrow is another day I thought. My answer came quickly without equivocation. Have blanket, will travel!

We were on our way in an hour. We headed South to our favorite trail. It was a trek that allowed a venture back into the timbers where the availability of periodic seclusion awaited. My trusty boots (K-Mart Yosemite's) served me well over a well-used six year period. Comfort and durability were major features in my decision to try them over the more costly name brands. It proved a good choice. My Yose' as I called them never failed me.

Jen was stunning in her earth-tone shorts and hikers with a light weight, modified knee sock. They were bright red of course; her favorite of favorites. Having walked for an hour and some, we decided to trek onto a location off of the pathway for a break. Once there, we devoured the well-prepared food. Red wine flowed a bit as well. We rested and dozed off slightly. The wind coming off the river was a welcome companion. The long overflow of the willow tree we lay under soothed and seduced us into an extended break. We made love beneath the blessing of this wondrous willow. It provided respite and protection from the razzle-dazzled life of the city. Her breasts were full, firm and flirtatious to my touch. My hands became one with them and rolled and responded with each ebb and flow of our incorporation into each other over and over again. We disregarded everything not a part of the rapture of two intermingling beings in the elongated moment of oneness.

Following the bath of endorphins, we talked about life, the mystery within and our deep gratitude for consciousness and for our relationship. We had been together now for nearly two years marked by numerous fun-filled experiences and glorious discoveries of each other wrapped in the desire to continue on without end or serious problem. We were a couple in love caught in the mystery of joyful relationship. We allowed room for the other devoid of control or ownership. Free spirits in ongoing entanglement galore. We hydrated ourselves and did a 180 back to my car. It was a typical, yet unbelievable time together. Yet, somehow both knew that each of us wanted more.

Jen was born and raised in India. She negotiated an easy blend of Buddhism and Western Transcendentalism as her compass. A most unusual orientation for a Physicist turned PhD in Therapeutic Psych. We were alike, yet different. That difference was never a problem for us. We knew and practiced the value of compromise. Perhaps it was simply open-mindedness in action that served us well. Heated discourse without anger. She was part Hindu and part British Colonial Overflow… she loved Keats, Shelley, and Coleridge. She also was an avid reader of Wordsworth and E.E. Cummings. The flourish of Jazz around the word did not escape her. Her fluency in French and success in common day Spanish were part of her lingual talents. Einstein was a hero to her. His bold declarations served as a mantra for her. She held forth on Quantum Mechanics, the parallels in Zen Buddhism, Taoism, principles of Physics, Brahman and African thought. The universal undefinable, yet observable phenomenon were magnets of attraction for her thoughts.

For me a quasi-persistent belief and continuous surrender to a force and/or intelligence beyond the normal human range was fine for me. I claimed no religion nor did I adhere to a single name for this being. Jen offered choices. My concern was focused less on the how, why, what and when and more on the who and identity in the personal and universal. The psyche, and how to manage its unfolding and manifestations for balance, happiness and health preoccupied me for my entire life. I was satisfied to teach and press minds; to get students to think and apply the brilliant techniques of psychology. Knowing the what goes with knowing when to use. The structure of the University and how it operated held little interest for me. Institutionalism held no attraction, period. The Transcendentalism of Thoreau and Emerson and Wordsworth was far more enticing. My orientation was near pure pragmatism. Simply go with what works.

Reality Therapy, Rational Emotive Therapy and Cognitive Therapy were cornerstones in my courses tracing the eternal development of the self. Behavior Modification was part of the curriculum but there was no tooting its value or usage. Trump cards were integrity, self-knowledge, open-minded response to life and its varied stimuli. Students embraced it fully at times, others simply asked if that material was going to be on the next test.

Education had begun to show signs of becoming a big business. Institutionalism bowed to "bigger-is-better" thinking, more improves score. If you want to be part of the splendid process you need to pay a lot of money for the sheepskin and the opportunities it delivers. The Ph.D. was a call card. It was the secret code to get you inside the loop. You simply need place it in your back pocket, partially displaying it for all eyes to see.

Sports not only helped contribute to sound minds. These programs were on the road to being monumental and a major source of revenue. But you needed to have the program in order to identify outstanding athletes in the country. The institution had to court and entice them to become one of its members. The payoff was exceptional. It was an excellent investment of time, energy and effort plus money.

The grass grew in its threat to go wild. A high school kid agreed to keep the lawn intact for the remaining days of summer. On the days the grass was to be cut there-on, I ate a late breakfast or had tacos and marguerites if the cut was in the afternoon.

My mind came to focus on the ways we humans act and yet, remain the same. We improve, move forward, become more caring while retaining contradicting traits like self-absorption, greed, violence and disregard for others. It was mind boggling for me. The noted progress recognized by historians, psychologists, archeologists and the academic community was oxymoronic in many ways. How is it possible for the American culture, for example, to demonstrate kindness and concern for the world's needs while simultaneously tolerating high levels of poverty and hunger of its own people. Incongruence seems to be woven into the fiber of America.

As an educator, my task was to help minds to open, blossom, expand awareness and stay grounded. Psychology trumpets positive thought, control, balance and productivity.

When merged with justice it produces honest, fair, and enjoyable experiences. No front-load agendas nor manipulation of others. This blend favors sharing and care. It addresses need and strives to satisfy. Intervention in order to bring remediation of known problems. This is pivotal, somehow the lower behavior patterns appear to be on a path of dominance.

World War II brought suffering and massive destruction. It likewise necessitated absolute co-operation and ultimate prosperity for most who were players in this earth-altering episode of mankind.

In our country, we rode the rails to growth and opportunity. We developed a first-class attitude and identity. We also ramped up and redeveloped our participation in Capitalism. And while we grew and prospered, we unintentionally became indifferent to the need and care of others. Welcome Mr. Greed and self servitude.

THE AWAKENING

An unplanned trip home for a week brought me back to Newark. My family members were adjusting to the loss of my paternal grandfather, who suffered a severe stroke at age 92. He had just celebrated a birthday. Not only was I close to him but thankfully, I had been regularly phoning him to stay in touch and give him the opportunity to see life through my meanderings and personal interests. We respected each other and I revered him. His death was a great loss to me, and I struggled to retain a balance while grieving. Tears and emotional surge were easily triggered by the recollection of the last time I saw him several months back. It was at a time when a short visit took place while driving to Philadelphia to participate in a conference for therapists. The distance between the two cities was marginal so I took advantage of the proximity before and after the conference to see my family. I most enjoyed time with my Gran Pa. He enjoyed a full life. Good health, strong family ties, a well-honed sense of dignity and a dry sense of humor marked his success as a human being. He was never not available to me whenever I was in Newark.

My grandfather had migrated to America earlier in the century from Lublin, Poland by way of Ellis Island and the welcoming gaze of the Statue of Liberty. He left shortly after World War I came to an end. As such, he escaped prior to the German and Soviet invasion of 1939. Polish Jews were the target of repression. He departed his homeland following increased threats by the Nazi movement to Germanize Lublin. In doing so he avoided the mass extermination of all Jews in his country. Gran Pa Matt dodged a lethal bullet.

Frequent were his stories of how it felt to escape the predictable Nazi purge of European Jews and embrace the sanctuary of freedom represented in Lady Liberty. Those who were caught in the Nazi grip were carted to concentration camps. Nearly all the Jews of Lublin were murdered. He truly made the right decision.

He lost his parents at an early age. His early developmental stage was a struggle, marked by various institutional living arrangements controlled by the State. On the one hand he had the semi security of safety wherein basic survival needs were satisfied. On the other, he lacked freedom to do what he pleased. He affirmed and strongly emphasized the value of freedom over security. Gran Pa Matt was a living testimony to the value of liberty. At the earliest opportunity he was on his way to the New World of hope and prosperity. While being processed at the port of entry in New York harbor, a mix up of some type took place. The surname he had been given by the Polish government, Lublin, was misrepresented as Lubin. And so, that became his official name, Matthew Lubin. Upon achieving citizenship, he began working as a laborer for a construction company. He was a fast learner and when he mastered basic English, he advanced to a foreman position. I continue to miss him.

Upon my return, Jen and I decided we were in need of a vacation. We booked a short trip south and soon after exiting the plane we were met by the soft balmy breeze of a Caribbean island. On our way to the resort we noticed a white crushed sandstone that provided a chalk-like environment. A vibrant jungle was becoming the Los Angeles freeway in the Caribbean. Graders and stone crushers boomed in uproarious blasts in a blended harmony with dust clouds. A surrealistic sight which marked the beginning of what was beautiful, dense-growth coastal greenery turned to cement pathways. High speed trucks sped by on the narrow roadway, eager to deliver their precious cargo to designated locations.

Massive, interlinking roadways traced their paths through enormous open and precise flatland surface. A foretell of airports and super highway access. A 360's of massive space in transition. The plan for the future of this region was manifesting. It was somewhat mesmerizing and sad to watch enormous change in action.

As we headed toward our destination, my mind focused on earlier visits to this land of splendor and enchantment. The glistening sun, relentless in fulfillment of its task, harkened a slower pace. Today, this radiant sphere functions as a task master. Work was to be done! The engineering of a modern road system. Crush, grumble and roll.

Few native people were seen in between passage through small village and hamlet that pock-marked the journey. The work area which seemed to encompass these habitats were populated by many hard-hat workers with mask-faced protection. The agents of material evolution. "Progress through growth and development," Western man's adornment. Ego pecking its way through the hazy natural state of grace. What assertiveness!

Upon arrival at the Oasis, as I called it, tequila welcomed us. Replenished by finger foods with salsa and bean dips, Jennifer and I showered together, had vigorous sex then slept for a while. Upon awakening we made love again. She was completely engaged in her love making. She gave herself totally and willingly received that which came back to her. She teased, toyed and then conquered with enduring embraces and full kisses. She understood and surrendered to the ebb and flow of partners in love. Sexual encounter with Jen was a complete entanglement without rule or limit. Basic consideration and appropriate concern for the other were at all times present. No exceptions. These moments were always tender and memorable if not magical.

Dreams, it seems, can become the doorway to keen perception. I had just witnessed a country in sharp transition. It was a country aspiring to leap into a loftier position in the second world tier (classification). I'm not sure it could ever attain first world status. It is most difficult to abandon the lower caste of a rigid ranking system. My dream that first evening entertained a vision of this beautiful country being absorbed by the USA. A new haven for those who would rest, bask and frolic in this new playground of soft breeze, blue waters and pleasant temperatures.

Americana. A position of world dominance had invaded this pristine realm of the tropics. The intended outcomes were quite obvious: capitalistic gains in this free market enterprise zone. A race for the better jockey positions marked an earlier period of development. This current surge rode in on a wave of corporate co-operatives. Partnerships and various mergers were the flavor of the day. Good-bye quaint village and fishnet handlers. Hello to the grandiose, the trek to monopolization of the highly favored territory. No globalization goals here. A plain and simple profit via the buyout of small ownership of land. What a scheme. "No Losers!" Yeah?

The mega companies were on the move. Keep the ball rolling south to the equator and beyond. There was to be no end to expansion and prosperity. Progress dictates development and benefit to all–especially the banks–there are no unforeseen problems. All is well. The next target: Antarctica?? Temp cycle from climates tropic to zero centigrade in five decades or less. Now that's progress!

As we motored back to the airport asphalt segregated the land in discriminate design. The road to be 'more traveled' in days to come was both picturesque and disturbing to me. More oil, tar and crushed stone replacing verdant pasture. A future supply of rubble trampled by car, truck, bus tours and other motorized vehicles was quite evident. Pity the planet.

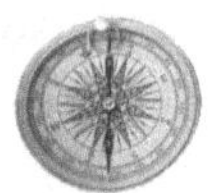

Seismic Social Change Ahead

Something had changed between us. She was somehow different. Her eyes continued to meet mine in open, accepting reciprocity. Non-judgmental was her gaze. What continued was a simple, involved interest in each other. This had always been the case with us. No questions, demands or deadlines. We just fit. Nevertheless, there was this something. I put my awareness to rest and concluded it to be nothing more than new unknowns to be explored and enjoyed. The tick of time would be the obvious unveiling.

We chatted briefly, then Jen said how much she liked these people of the island. "I admire and respect their simplicity and kindness. These qualities are absent at the university," she continued.

"I long for this simplicity and purposeful life style. No waste or aggressive agendas to deal with. Just live and enjoy life without all the neon and freon to pave the way. Live to be happy and enjoy. Forget the frills and thrills. Do as the French "Joie de la vie.""

My response was both subtle and appropriate.

"You've experienced a culture on the verge of going over the edge. It is no longer in transition. These people have tumbled into the modern age with all the capitalistic, free, democratized behaviors. It's most difficult to ignore if one wants a piece of the economic pie. In a way there is no way out. It appears the dominant pattern. Go along or be trampled."

She shot back with strong facial expression "You are much too calculating. You weigh everything out. You miss the beauty of diverse style and unique practices, and the independent exercise of choice."

I pondered her point, then uttered "this is not the either/or, what is present is the both/and occurrence. One need not completely abandon what one believes and lives for, one simply goes along to get along so to speak. Though not really. I agree that much is lost in this massive transition. Nevertheless, one can live in Rome without hailing Caesar. This was what was to happen. Or it can happen! Who knows?"

Jen appeared puzzled. She was quick to respond "Every human being is faced with a decision. A choice to be swept into the frenzied, fast-paced life style of America the beautiful or follow the beat of one's own heart. Somehow the two do not blend. They exist on parallel lines with periodic contact. The same streets are traveled, the same H2O is used and both listen to similar music, watch TV and shop the same groceries and retail stores. But, no blending regardless of apparent intermingle."

A broad resilient smile filled her face as we continued on toward our destination. The discussion was interrupted by a pit stop and grabbing some refreshments at a multi-service plaza. Little did I know that this was to be our last trek of any type. We were done at trips end. Prosit!

The flight home was uneventful. Upon completing the tedious trek through customs and walk to the car we drove to a small restaurant, had some light food and retired for the night. Later, as the new school year approached, we found ourselves slowly parting ways. The sizzle and magnetic pull had vanished.

As our relationship endured this wobble for several months, we realized that it had been a good road to travel together, but ever increased detours and unrepaired potholes galore left their damage and emotional scar. We knew that no patch or redo would salvage the tottering connect as it continued to waffle and wane. The wanton rapport closed itself with the participants searching out new pathways. Upon graduation she was to accept a teaching position in the peaks of Colorado. I obviously clung to my tenured position.

The days and weeks that followed the break up with Jennifer were both painful and liberating. We had been together in an off-on and some-times up-down and around in a multi-faceted relationship. The peaks basked in ecstasy. An experience much-like a most delectably satisfying, well prepared favorite meal. The valleys drilled beyond the discomfort in the depths of Death Valley. This dip-thrust engagement demanded heroic patience and a highly cultivated discipline.

Jennifer was in many ways my intellectual equal. At times she exceeded my level. These were times when she would capitalize on the "superior moment" as I called them.

She had a quick wit, sharp tongue and was never hesitant to go for the jugular. I've always protected my neck even when I stretch it out there when asserting an unconventional idea, strong conviction or an immovable commitment to a political issue.

She used her training in yoga to nurture a supple mind with boggling statements and a Newtonian reflex for bouncing back in reaction to accusation and aggressive criticism. I was always permitted to make a positive suggestion, but the rule of thumb was be ready to duck and defend when you've opted to criticize—even when constructive in design. She harbored a low tolerance for such action. Jen always made certain I crashed and burned when I was flying high or gaining an edge in our quarrels. She did this with poignant tone or with fury. Her "rave-on" frequently morphed into "rage-on". So be it.

The Caribbean trip had stimulated questions of interest to me. Was being the Alpha in a group or for that matter, a culture, the ultimate objective in human living? Why was there so much and so little shared? Was human greed a natural tendency? How might justice and balance be attained? These were queries on the philosopher's plate, but the Alpha and greed issues sat well on the clinical psychologist's platter. These were concerns I continued to think about. For whom does the bell toll anyway?

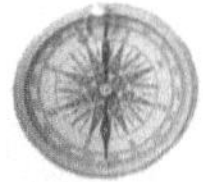

DG. Esposito

White Mountains Trek

The remainder of the school year was unremarkable. Continued studious work brought kudos from students and much boredom to my mind. I continued to tussle with the absence of Jennifer.

Time ticks slowly when you lose love. Late summer brought increased temperatures and restless feelings. This annual recurrence prompted the need to move, to explore, to do something extraordinary. Then it was back to the paces of another school year. The White Mountains of New Hampshire typically trumped the Adirondacks and Catskills of New York. Mount Washington at 6,288 feet was a refreshing change from the modest yet beautiful ranges of the Alleghenies. The trip crossed over much of Pennsylvania, into New York at Port Jarvis. We followed the scenic route 209 to Kingston where we hopped onto route 87 north, through Albany and entered Vermont at Ticonderoga. We had some food and slept in a small cabin in the Green Mountain National Forest.

The next morning, we zigzagged across the state to White River Junction and stepped into New Hampshire via Lebanon to Route 93 north into the White Mountains. We were greeted by the "Man of the Mountains" (semblance of a stone head) shortly after entering the White Mountain Natural Forest. Next was a rejuvenating drive full of eye-catching vistas and surprising shifts in the land. We camped out overnight in this wondrous untampered forest.

My travel mate, an ex-college girl-friend, who, like me, enjoyed the free life. We both were wanderers in a land of plenty. She had not married. She took a job with the Carnegie Institute as a History Associate. The job was a one-year position subsidized by the federal government. Jessica was beautiful, intelligent and very sexy. She also enjoyed having a good time. To be with her was to have fun, to laugh and cavort. You would never take her for a history buff. We met at a popular coffee shop down near Duquesne University a few months back. We quickly renewed our relationship. It was a natural follow up to our college romance. No real need to say, Jessica was a highly favored travel companion. She also liked the percolator like sound of my Saab. On occasion, she operated the noble vessel.

Jessica was athletic and had become an avid hiker since we last met a chunk of years back. Her hiking gear showed moderate usage. The boots were "all terrain" which would be most useful on our assent to Mt. Washington via Tuckerman's Trail. An 8.4-mile eye grabbing series of vistas. The hike reached 4300 feet and offered a formidable challenge to legs/bodies not regularly involved in vertical ascent. A full half day climb.

The trail was busy on the day we set out to tackle this monolith. Most traffic was headed to the base. These one-way hikers had taken the cog-rail to the top then lunged into the descent. We marveled at the diversity among those clomping downwards. They were rookies, older veterans, the time-limited trekker and so on. Most were friendly as they passed by offering a verbal greeting, head nod or a simple smile. Others did not acknowledge us but were locked into concentration on down-ward movement. There were frequent calling out to alert others to difficult spots that could be dangerous. On occasion we would pass those who rested before their next assault. At other times, hikers trudged their way past Jessica and me onto the summit.

On one of our stops we found a waterfall and a small pond that allowed bathing. Several groups had passed us prior to our stop. The place was without others. We capitalized on the opportunity. Off with garments and boots and a cannon-ball entry into the pond. A taste of Nirvana? An ice-cold enlightenment! Two small groups noticed our frolic but kept a military pace upward. Being lovers of peace and not war, we slowed the pace of our love making and giggled like high school kids "getting-it-on" in the girls' locker room without anyone ever finding out. Endorphins flowed ever so freely. "Let's never let go," Jessica said as I nodded in trance-like agreement.

We rejoined the migration upward. Along the way we noted the bruises and minor scratches sustained on the trail thanks to the slip, trip and misstep. The view of the ravine was spectacular. This escarpment continues to have snow from the previous winter. The remnant of blown snow stacked several hundred feet up the steep face on the Northeast base. What an astonishing sight in mid-August.

We reached the timber line and embraced the treeless rockscape. Later in the climb we reached the last 1500 feet or so. This was a near vertical hand knee crawl up and over large rocks that had been dislodged and tumbled down in a confused yet organized disarray. It was a genuine granite and hard rock haven.

The summit reached brought cheers from onlookers and a welcome embrace from Jessica. It was mutual jubilation and appreciation for a fete well done. Jessica frequently caught my eye as each gently gazed into the yet unknown appeal of the other. The climb had taken us (frolic included) ten hours.

We rested with a sense of serene satisfaction. We took in some nourishment and hydrated ourselves in prep for the descent. As we approached and turned onto the trail an older man in his 70s greeted us. We gave way to this grey-haired gent, who gleefully asserted that he had just run all the way up the trail. Wow! The easier, faster trail melted away beneath the well-placed foot. It appeared to disappear more quickly as we worked our way to the halfway house, where we rested once more. The final steps to the bottom were eager and carefully engineered. O terra firma!

The entire experience was fatiguing yet laced with unforgettable moments of "wows." "look at this." and endless hugs, kisses and hand clasping. A superb joy combined with the unequivocal desire, if not, firm promise to do it again. It had been a true adventure. There was no set plan 'cept climb the Tuckerman Trail at the ravine and recreate the whatever.

Since neither of us smoked cigarettes, we celebrated our wondrous journey by lighting a joint as we gave thanks for a safe return to the level plain. A slow leg-ache stroll to the Saab ensued.

We slept under the stars at a camp on the northern tip of the National Forest. A cool beautiful late evening sky greeted us upon arrival. A quick bathroom stop, followed by some nourishing snacks, then a restful, open air sleep upon the ground.

Morning brought breakfast at a nearby diner. Coffee, juice, bacon, eggs and home fries surrounded by toast was the call. It was a typical mountaineer's breakfast. The weather continued to be warm and sunny with timeless breezes. We responded to the inner call nudging us along. By noon we were in Maine at Bethel. We motored down route 26 as it twisted its way into Lewiston/Ashburn then turned South onto 495 and headed to Portland. As we carved our way through the wondrous terrain, talk centered on the seafood at South Portland. We rehearsed menus as appetites loomed large. We considered a ferry ride to Nova Scotia but decided against doing so. Open sea was great. Fresh seafood and rest were better.

Shellfish, shellfish and more shellfish. The food at the pier was outstanding. No bells, whistles. Keep it simple. Steamed, fried, baked or broiled clams, shrimp, crab, lobster and oysters were the order of the day for a few days. Local brew accompanied the festivities. "Portland, you must really have been something in your day," I said. Jessica nodded as she sunk her teeth into a lobster the size of Manhattan.

On the road again we paused for a couple of hours to watch kayaks and canoes exit the Saco River at Biddeford. River to Ocean. What a trip! Jessica suggested we spend a night in Hampton Beach in New Hampshire. We found a hotel very close to the beach.

Energized by a good night's sleep we strolled the beach before the sun pierced the horizon. Her hair was loose and freely partnered with dawn's firm wind, which embraced and twirled it in dance-like patterns. She was totally immersed in the steady flow, her face aglow in the spontaneous encounter as if a glass of cool water had quenched her thirst in the late but very hot sun. She was obviously reinvigorated and stated so, "wow, that feels so good. I could stand or sit facing this breeze of fair winds. Let's spend more time here. What's say?"

"I don't know, we were scheduled to be in NYC by tomorrow afternoon."

"O come on now, we found a great place to recharge," she pleaded.

"We do have many miles and travel hours to go, you do recall."

No response followed.

After a pregnant silence, we chose to allow the endorphins to flow and gave thanks to the wind gods.

To hell with keeping in line with a trip agenda.

This was now an adventure.

Go with the wind. Bend with the road. Eat when hunger calls. Sleep only when energy is totaled out. The joy is in the journey, not the time, nor the calendar (some of the time). But this day belonged to no clock or calendar.

While looking at Jessica's hair sauntering about, my mind remembered other encounters with wind in the mountains, the open plains, on water and simply strolling on campus. The wind is a mighty healer of varied malady. It cures headaches, recalibrates the mind, and helps solve problems. It distracts from pain, cools body sense, warms the soul, and settles nerves. As well it emboldens courage, refreshes the source of balance, and brings clarity of mind. When wind howls and whistles in the ear one can foresee the future somewhat. Wind is clairvoyant. An awareness devoid of words, crystallizes in its alert. I have been healed by wind. It is my medicine. It has removed or reduced corruption in the bone, sanitized the skin, calmed the heart and its fluctuating beat. It scatters the petty, insignificant physical complaints pivoting on pain. The wind teaches silence and nurtures good will: "he who feels good, shares the good." Wind alters mindset and galvanizes attitude. This rejuvenator of wellness, be it in mountains, plains, valleys, lakes, rivers, oceans, farm lands, deserts and caverns is one and the same while manifesting differently in astounding prance. The westerly's, tropical, arctic, and Himalayan winds are sibling or cousins depending on origin. A close friend of the sun it fulfills one of its tasks by delivering moisture, oxygen, cool-dry temps and churning the many oceans and seas. Oh, to be a sailor, at times, is my only dream.

The wind spawns ideas, purifies plans and can beat the living hell out of you. It is a good friend. It can also be a formidable foe when in a blustery mood. Wind is most accommodating when piloting a sail boat cutting through waves. Without the wind all is static, where the inept prevails, leaves do not scatter nor decorate the landscape. In its absence all is still, silent and joyless except for the dark cloud, the rain drops and water everywhere in a chaos of dance begun in a shallow stream. Rain, rain, can anyone explain when hydrogen met oxygen? And to what degree was wind involved in such an encounter.

I give thanks to have wind as my medicine. Thrusts of air can place us into a trance, be lost in its intoxicating influence as it carts us away and into different worlds that we are vaguely aware of. These welcome exposures are a tonic for my brain, natural tranquilizers to wearied mind, a salve for aching joint and muscle. An absolutely splendiferous venture into unknown, yet, not regularly visited domains. It was at that moment, when Jessica called me to watch a boy raising a kite to the sky, that my mind quickly but reluctantly disengaged from my love for and penetrating thought about the wonder of a bird soaring on the wind. What envy!

We took a swim and helped the sun usher-in dusk. Melodic sounds and some lyrics from the Beatles bounced around in my head, "… because the world is round…" As dusk approached Jess called me to a nearby stack of beach chairs and umbrellas. She knew it would provide a perfect haven for privacy. I approached her discovery in a nonchalant way and feigned little interest. She laughed at me and brought me to the sand then rolled over on top of me as we found our way to that familiar rapture. She was most playful that evening and enticed several encores. My performance was supported by the tumbling and crashing of waves just yards from where we lay. There was, once again, a certain juvenile aspect to the accomplishment. We had performed an act of togetherness not welcome in public.

The Saab powered us down and through Massachusetts, Rhode Island into New York City where we found a great little place to rest and recreate for a few days. We thought about attending a rock concert at Madison Square Garden but recognized the need for sleep. Howard Johnson in the Bronx served us well. Two days later, following extended sojourns in Greenwich Village and Central Park, we headed west by way of the George Washington Bridge onto route 80. We zoomed past familiar land marks as the Saab powered in and through New Jersey. No stops in my home state, but time at the Delaware Water Gap proved refreshing as we marveled at the sheer beauty of the area. The Delaware River serves as border for Jersey and Pennsylvania. Then, back on the road, we entered the amazing Poconos, which, in the summer was enticing and beautiful as possible. It was a no stop trek through this mountainous, water laced land. Jessica was due back at the Carnegie Institute the next day. We motored along and were surprised to see the large number of deer that met their end while crossing this high-speed expressway. Jessica, aghast, with hand to her mouth muttered, "What a slaughter! Will it ever stop!" "Who knows? This is a new highway. It will take a while for the deer to figure out new ways to cross. What a miserable shame in the name of progress."

Jess was bred in a metro area in southern Maryland, with minimal contact with animal life outside the Chesapeake Bay.

Pittsburg showed up six hours later in time for Jessica to make work. She was a conscientious employee who would complete her contract in three months. We saw each other regularly as the Fall semester unfolded into late November. It marked our last time together. Jessica returned to her work at Carnegie, but shortly thereafter, transferred to a position in NYC at the Natural History Museum.

The Spring Semester was on its way to be another unremarkable path to be on. The school year rambled by, as mental fatigue and the desire to disengage from the campus centered life drove me to look elsewhere for respite. But where? A deepening restlessness loomed within me so I researched available psych conferences and other updated training sessions. My choice was appropriate thanks to a last-minute cancellation on the roster two weeks from my initial search. I leapt at the opportunity to participate.

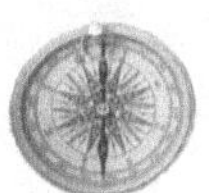

SUFFICE THE DAY

It was that morning. I mean that kind of morning that gives rise to desire, appetite and drive. It was a day that fuels awareness and goal. My thoughts were rapid flow and fluid. Pen to hand led to theory and hypothesis. A high produce day of writing.

This day was a mind swirl, a seamless quilt with full spectral color. A conscious delight speckled with existential angst. Adler, Jung, Karen Sullivan, and others were reviewed, my mind flooded with Rollo May, Reward Theory, and Goal-oriented Theory. Gordon Allport, Carl Rogers, Herbert Maslow and so on… I thought of the one and the many, harmony and oneness, the integration of all things and the separateness of the self in ego disconnect from others. It was invigorating.

A psychologist is a positive light, one who resolves pain, harm and suffering. He is a guide to carve new pathways out of self-doubt, confusion, emotional entanglement and other forms of incarceration. He encourages dreams and stimulates imagination and belief. The architect of self-confidence and reasonable risk taking. He diffuses conflict, creates options and models the way to liberation.

The distillation of my thoughts, in what was an endless moment in consciousness, centered on health as wholeness. Health is the integration of the self and the fullness of being in balance. No edge or heaviness nor amoeba spread. There is orientation and purpose. A cohesive flow without stutter, misstep, nor glitch. It is the ongoing gathering of all components, head, heart, emotion, psyche, intuition and gratitude. The acceptance of life marked by a genuine appreciation of living.

I walked in the sunrise of this given day. Light was my guide. Brilliant red, soft orange and silent blues echo each other's call. The early breeze foretells events of the day. That which was yet to come. A California morning on the beach of Big Sur. A crash smash along the shore speaks of change and playfulness. Stress departs unveiling peace and contentment. The open shore is a gateway, a window to wonder, a re-entry into the self. Perhaps, the wonder of wonders. Who are we? Why are we here? Is there a purpose in consciousness?

In the midst of this lucid wonderment I surprisingly remembered and or recognized that I was at the Esalen Institute in the summer of 1966.

The Problem

My private therapeutic practice kept me busy into the Fall and early winter. A trip to the other side of the state provided a holiday of skiing.

They do not go down!

Defiant conviction. The perennial detour of progress and health. A problem is a problem of a problem. Cause me havoc, bring some pain, the problem generates loss yet promotes growth. Amidst the turmoil, a problem offers opportunity to improve, find new paths or reverse, search and/or alter the present situation. It calls for creativity and serious thought. And let's not forget effort and self-searching.

Janie and Carl were newlyweds vacationing in the Poconos when I met them. Our first encounter took place on the slopes of Jack Frost in the NE section of Pennsylvania. After a full morning of continuous runs down the intermediate slopes, I had decided to go for the "Big One." However, on my first attempt my right ski hit something that threw me into a tumble to the left side. Several rolls followed the fall as the slide down the slope found momentum.

It was Carl who clasped my arm and spun me round pulling me out of the slide to safety. Jane, at his side, quickly assisted to help me to my feet. Actually, it was a one-foot stand since one ski remained on my left foot. I was shaken and a bit dazed from the tumble. I offered no argument in refusal of their help.

Back inside the lodge I thanked them for their kind and timely help. It was at that time that I sensed a glitch in their relationship. Months later it became increasingly clear how broad based that glitch was.

They were from the Pittsburg area as well, so plans were made for them to look me up some time. And following several rounds of cognac and some snacks they returned to the slopes and I to my room for some rest. After a short nap, a hot shower nudged discomfort away

I later rejoined my date who had taken an afternoon tour of the beautiful Pocono Mountain area. We had several drinks and enjoyed a wonderfully prepared NY strip.

We closed out our day with a night cap in our room and mused the events of the day. Early next morning we turned our vehicle onto route 80 west and motored home. Linda chose to stay at my place for a few days since her holiday continued for a time yet. She always took a respite from her work as a social psychologist or, as she preferred, a psychiatric social worker. Mid-January proved to be an ideal time to step away from daily contact with retired wealthy individuals in need of psychiatric help. We met 5 years back while working in a retirement community. We continued to take a January weekend ski trip if/when each of us was free of an intimate relationship. Sometimes it worked out and other times it never took place.

Several months later my office reported a new request for marriage counseling. The couple turned out to be Jane and Carl. The marriage situation had deteriorated since we last spoke in the Poconos. The primary concern focused on increased conflict, accusations of declining love and a common life marked by ongoing misery. Jane's main complaint targeted Carl's domineering ways which she explained as over-controlling and smothering. She felt he did not respect her and infrequently acknowledged her achievements as a real estate agent. Signs of the marital fracture surfaced early in that first appointment. Jane was obviously hurt and felt underappreciated. She was a young woman on the verge of bolting the marriage.

Carl was a manager in a highly successful grocery chain in Western PA and Cleveland areas. He was executive material, flaunted a business management degree from Penn State University. He was narrow minded, had a strong sense of his personal viewpoint and given to having his own way at work, at home and certainly in directing his wife's behavior. His complaint claimed Jane was overly sensitive, limited in her experience of the world, and that she constantly complained about what she saw as his controlling ways.

I had a policy in my practice not to work with friends, family or romantic partners. Since we had no relations other than the brief encounter on the ski slope back in January, I decided to work with them.

There is no need to explain the arduous process of sorting out how individual feelings and emotions were clarified and aligned to truth and intention. How conflict resolution promoted positive change and the fascinating phenomenon of a person who simply chooses not to change for the better. Suffice to know that the relationship sputtered and staggered for six additional months marked by periodic growth, some serious back-slides and several destructive infidelities. Their common insight that the relationship was no longer worth saving with serious hurt orbiting their lives and the obvious truth that neither one chose to expend the energy to salvage the severely damaged marriage, a mutual decision was made to end the marriage and each went the road that was most appealing.

And so goes the work of a therapeutic psychologist. Endless hours of diligent, objective mirroring to the client visions of herself founded on expressed images, shared feeling, hopes, frustration, fears and anger. The clarification of what prevents them from attaining what they want and hope for. What is needed to successfully acquire or do what it is they want with suggestions to aid and maintain their perspective in their efforts to bring about desirable/necessary change in one's life. As mentioned earlier, I loved my therapeutic involvements which gave me a sense of livelihood satisfaction and a much-needed fuel for the classroom. The two practices worked together for mutual improvement and ongoing challenge. Continuous challenge is vital, and therefore a necessity for a vibrant, healthy and balanced life, both personal and professional. My life was enriched in responding to the challenge. My success in these combined involvements gave me a sense of contentment and satisfaction. I was at peace with myself and the world surrounding me. I had worked through my own divorce years back. Liberation from the guilt freed me to live in the present with energy and clear goals. There no longer were negative issues impacting my life. I lived with deliberation, planned fun time into my busy schedule and always managed to have great companionship. Life was good.

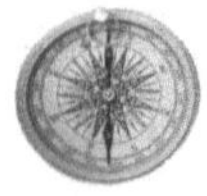

ON IT GOES

From my office window on the fourth floor I saw it unfold. It was both impressive and somewhat startling at the same time. Students put into action a well thought out plan. It involved a nationwide anti-Vietnam War protest. Campus entrances were blocked by large timbered trees. Faculty, administration personnel, staff and student commuters were prevented entrance onto the campus. It would prove to be a significant protest that drew clearer attention to the moral unacceptability of this war. Local media showed up to provide vivid coverage of this brazen yet brilliant student strategy.

Since I had biked onto the campus from my nearby apartment without using main entrances, I hadn't noticed the set up until I became aware of controlled shouting and administrative commands. The welcome distraction from my early morning, robot-like grading of term papers was astounding. Resident students were locked in quasi consent on the issue. There was, however, the common banter among those with different viewpoints. The main cafeteria swelled to capacity and proved to be the venue for a political exchange with much cheering and booing. Attempts by senior faculty members in their appeal for a more reasonable approach paled in comparison to the impassioned rhetoric barked by protest supporters. It was a momentous event. I was total observer of the occasion even though my personal views were previously expressed in the classes I taught.

This masterful plan to nudge polarization on a world-wide impact issue had varying consequences. Some student leaders were arrested, colleges and universities complained of semester disruption and corresponding cleanup costs, the media had its new focus and the government ignored the outrageous and un-American clamor.

The continued escalation of US troops into the conflict to support the crumbling South Vietnam government was true to script to halt the spread of Communism. In the hearts and minds of the North Vietnam, this was an intrusion into their private matters. They wanted a unified country under one flag. As such, a relentless flow of foot soldiers manifested this deep feeling. The foot path taken was aptly called the Ho Chi Minh Trail.

He orchestrated the strategy which proved to be more than a counter assault to the bombardment by US aircraft. The Napalm, nor sophisticated technologically-advanced weapons had little impact in this dense jungle habitat. I was not surprised several years later when our government drew down troops and recognized Vietnam as a country engaged in Civil War. The will of the North Vietnamese could not be thumped. American ego was bruised. It marked our first loss in an impressive history of military success. Conflict at home continued. All was not yet done; if peace were to prevail.

It had been a bloody tumult for a decade and some. The U.S. had been experiencing ongoing enormous internal conflict beginning with the birth of the Civil Rights Movement, the assassination of JFK. This unrest expanded in the escalation of troops in Vietnam, the assassinations of MLK and RFK. The endless saga of young men losing limbs and life in Vietnam and the rise of Post-Traumatic Stress Syndrome fueled war protesters and raised doubt in American minds about the legitimacy of this conflict. Clergy and educators and several congressional members took the lead in declaring the war immoral. Hawks waged on in opposition with Doves. Conservative views lobbied for the war's continuation. Liberals called us to a clearer perspective.

This conflict, co-joined with the Civil Rights push, raised questions focused on American standards, a newly formed vision of the world as one, a growing sense of woman's rights and an enormous thrust towards economic power gave rise to a wave of discontent in a stormy sea. Our world was undergoing rapid change and significant tumult. It marked the rise of world companies, global markets and the broad acceptance of Capitalism. This gigantic rumble rattled the world, severed comfort zones and awakened the minds of many to a new world dawning. It permeated music, novels, news columns, the proverbial TV-Radio Talk Shows. The shift had begun. The new paradigm revealed itself.

In retrospect, the period was much like the confluence of many contributory streams flowing into the heart of the river. Flower children in opposition to the materialistic power group, minorities surge toward enhancing their rights, the encroaching rise of technology and a redis-covered reverence for the earth, mind expansion, and respect for what was simple, natural and common permeated the continent and spilled somewhat into the world.

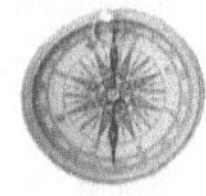

Sun and Wind Always Heal

Drawn to something in dawn's sparkled light, we quickly focused our attention on the fuzzy movement through the back-tent window. It might have been a deer or some other sizeable animal. Black bears are frequently encountered in the Cumberland Mountains of Maryland. This camping trip was a necessary get-a-way, a mental health holiday.

The spring semester brought me the typical fatigue and weary spirit feeling. This experience catapulted me into a break-free mentality. The need to regroup and rebalance became dominant. I sought fresh air, seductive winds and freedom from noise and tumult. The private campground offered just what I needed, no schedule to follow; open sky and the rejoining with nature.

We took the most remote site available. A scenic patch of grass with a view of the valley below. There was no picnic table. Instead, a fallen large maple uprooted three years earlier served as sitting area and table top. A ready-made shallow pit became the location (carefully) for our fire. We placed ancient stones around the pit and reveled at the accomplishment.

Setting up was easy. My dome style tent took form as we tethered it as we drove the final two stakes into the ground. Kindling was gathered and soon after we had a cozy fire hot enough to brew fresh coffee. There is nothing that compares to being in the mountains in early spring with a bustling fire. Coffee and food followed. Wood for the evening fire came to us without great effort.

We strolled the general area for a few minutes and discovered we were removed from other campsites. It was exactly what each of us needed after the long winter, dry heat and stale classroom air. The open, fresh and ever-present newness of the outdoors in early Spring was enthusiastically embraced and relished. We were alive! We were alone and entertained by natures surging beauty. All of it free under nature's canopy.

The late afternoon fire welcomed us with an arc of warmth and enough heat to roast up a rack of baby-back ribs. The ribs were coupled with French bread and a bottle of Merlot. Nirvana was near by… There is something about red wine and evening fire that resonates deep within our psyche. Perhaps they are part of the archetype package. Whatever the case, the experience is woven into the DNA fiber. Without exception, the combination spawns a euphoric mood. Euphoria is wonder. The totality of conscious awareness and sensate response to the activity of night, fire light, wind and silence.

All was well in this campsite of the first star-filled night. We embraced, kissed with joy in our heart and eyes. We then quickly found our way back to the tent and retired. We were a bit tired but totally renewed and regenerated. Needless to say, the undisturbed sleep that followed was mind enhancing.

Last evening was majestic. It called us to gaze in exquisite excitement at the varied clusters of stars. We guessed planets and constellations. We spotted several meteors.

The splendor of the clear night sky with illuminated dots and specs was unforgettable. Over and again the lights appeared to speak, calling us to a not yet seen, nor understood vista. Their effort to share secrets of the universe illuminated and astounded and faded into silence. Nevertheless, we had been dazzled by the spectacular display of the unfathomable black caress. We knew we had more to learn about Gaia and its place in the universe. The event deepened our appreciation of mystery in the galaxy. Izzy and I were filled with a profound gratitude for being a part of this wondrous experience.

Morning thrust its precious light on our fragile presence calling us to participate in the new day. A deep yawn and energetic stretch of muscle and tendon eagerly chased fatigue off and into the still darkened forest. This day was for recreation and relish. There would be no time for tiredness. A lazy river flowed within which governed pace and involvement. There was no need for unnecessary action or quicksilver antic. The river's call of the day was to be slow and easy. Lay it all back for a while. We lacked nothing. There was only energy and elation.

Discovery, rediscovery of simple pebbles, stones and sundrenched wood were the order of this day. We continued the adventure. There was much laughter, storytelling and sharing anew. Evening fires were marked by reflection, recaptured memories and clarification of wants, needs and goals. These were simple moments, filled with unexplainable connect and mutual exploration of our past, present and perhaps the to-be- possible-future.

We spoke not of probability, only possibilities. An Al Camus perspective was a frequent focus as the flames of the fire captured our imagination and mesmerized our spirits. We were alive, we were young, we chose to commune with nature, and we took advantage of this opportunity.

Izzy was a pragmatist with a well-prepared mind. English and literature were her main interest. Her conviction was Pantheistic in its orientation. She found the divine in every drop of moisture and the slow easy flow of the breeze. Open minded and most accepting of life as it unfolded to her, she obviously was a joy to be with. She was quick to adopt a different view on topics discussed. A mature sense of belonging without much questioning prompted her vision. She tended to tease out the best of the best in me. Done with an unavoidable smile and sparkle in the eye, Isabel was a teacher, visionary and very beautiful companion for any and all occasions. Uniqueness marked each breathe she took.

We continued the adventure for three more days then headed back to Pittsburg. We both had Monday morning classes.

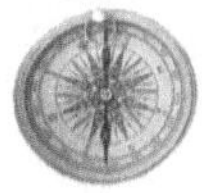

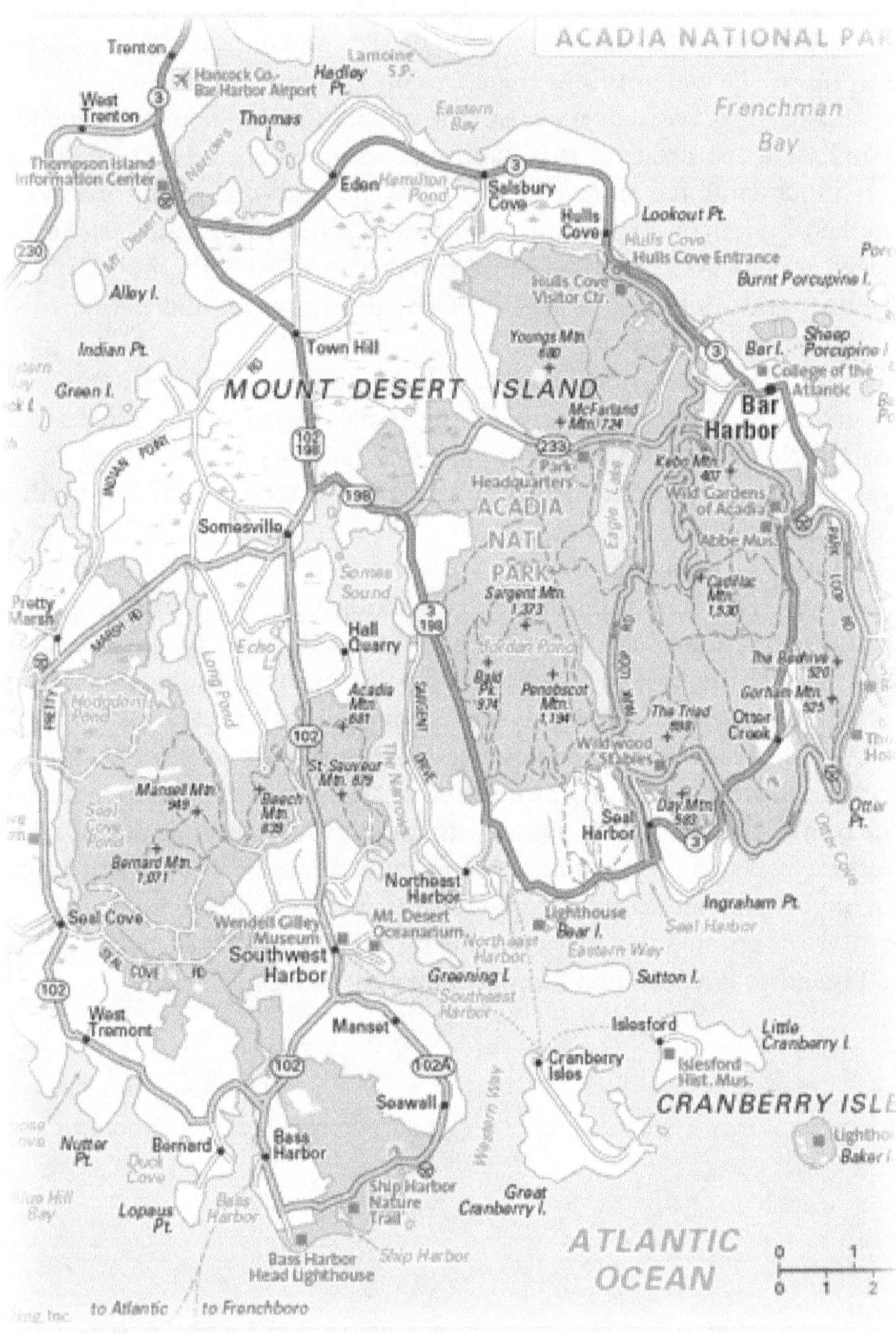
Trenton
Hancock Co.-Bar Harbor Airport
Hadley Pt.
Lamoine S.P.
West Trenton
Thomas I.
Eastern Bay
Frenchman Bay
Thompson Island Information Center
Mt. Desert Narrows
Eden
Hamilton Pond
Salsbury Cove
Hulls Cove
Lookout Pt.
Hulls Cove
Hulls Cove Entrance
Burnt Porcupine I.
Alley I.
Hulls Cove Visitor Ctr.
Youngs Mtn. 680
Sheep Porcupine I.
Indian Pt.
Bar I.
College of the Atlantic
Green I.
MOUNT DESERT ISLAND
Town Hill
McFarland Mtn. 724
Bar Harbor
233
Park Headquarters
Kebo Mtn. 407
Somesville
ACADIA NATL PARK
Wild Gardens of Acadia
Abbe Mus.
Somes Sound
Sargent Mtn. 1,373
Eagle Lake
Pretty Marsh
Cadillac Mtn. 1,530
Hall Quarry
Jordan Pond
Long Pond
Echo Lake
Acadia Mtn. 681
Bald Pk. 974
Penobscot Mtn. 1,194
The Bee Hive 520
Hodgdon Pond
St. Sauveur Mtn. 679
The Narrows
The Triad
Gorham Mtn. 525
Otter Creek
Mansell Mtn. 949
Beech Mtn. 839
Wildwood Stables
Seal Cove Pond
Day Mtn. 583
Otter Pt.
Bernard Mtn. 1,071
Seal Harbor
Northeast Harbor
Ingraham Pt.
Seal Cove
Wendell Gilley Museum
Mt. Desert Oceanarium
Lighthouse Bear I.
Seal Harbor
Southwest Harbor
Northeast Harbor
Eastern Way
West Tremont
Greening I.
Sutton I.
Manset
Southeast Harbor
Islesford
Little Cranberry I.
Cranberry Isles
Islesford Hist. Mus.
Seawall
CRANBERRY ISLES
Nutter Pt.
Bernard
Bass Harbor
Western Way
Lighthouse Baker I.
Duck Cove
Great Cranberry I.
Lopaus Pt.
Bass Harbor
Ship Harbor Nature Trail
ATLANTIC OCEAN
Bass Harbor Head Lighthouse
Ship Harbor
to Atlantic
to Frenchboro
0   1   2

Expect the Unexpected
"Separation, Loss and Retool"

"Carry on and don't waiver" became a daily intent. From morning until the moon glared in disappointment with the late evening sky. There was no turning back or opting out of the difficult and/or awkward experiences. I was well dressed in modern style and my nutritional needs were satisfied by the best of entrées. Beef and seafood were top choices with occasional selections of Italian platters and a good red wine. But I sensed a certain loss of interest on my part. The feeling of being swallowed by a whirlpool of indifference became overbearing.

The level of activity was a friend to my body weight. I hadn't always benefited from a healthy metabolism. However, the recent addition of tennis proved to be a timely ally.

Mid-section excess began its departure and my creative juices beckoned energy and more focus. There was noticeable weight loss and the once familiar feeling and function of being slender returned. My clothing fit better, and my gait showed buoyancy and bounce.

I enjoyed a series of mini accomplishments. There were fewer aches and a new found sense of the old times which were marked by good times, happy memories and a high level of function. Central to this period was frequent travel and micro trips balanced by several outstanding journeys. Today was a recall of what had been, and it gave clear indication of promptly returning. A significant transition was underway.

The materialistic, scientific, technological, bio-chemical revolution was addictive in its utter appeal and promise of a better, longer and more fulfilling life. The glitter of specialization erased the full view, the gestalt and the macro. There was no whole, only the parts. The diets, exercise programs, and mental gurus multiplied quickly. It was disquieting and seemed to me to be oxymoronic to revere individuality (the autonomous person) while seduced into compliance.

So many of my colleagues were in the rigid, negative, and irritating posture. They overly criticized political decisions and student attitude and antic. Educators always eager to express fatigued book-based perspectives on any and all subjects. I needed to get out. Too much intellectualizing does, in fact, promote dullness in a man. Wonder and a certain type of madness called me to adventure. Away then to a new location and a different style of taking a breath in and releasing one out. The situation unfolded quickly and heralded a trip with itinerary.

This was the situation I abandoned. I left it behind and moved on.

Immediately following my resignation from the university, I relocated to Northern Maine. This location was not the result of research and a well-constructed plan. It came about following a leisurely stroll through the southern borders of Canada with brief stops in Toronto and Montreal. The crossover at Buffalo served as an existential passing from an old pattern into a new, but not yet known new one. Upon entering Maine, I remembered the raw beauty of its rocky shores and the wondrous vistas of earth, sea and sky. Decision made. No more location quest.

Upon arrival I began writing on a daily basis. The writing was journal-like addressing my dreams, hopes, challenges, failures and insight concerning my health, feelings and my attitude toward everything and everybody I'd had commerce with. It was liberating and most rewarding. I also wrote about professional observation both as a psychologist and educator. The overstress on knowledge and the general need for compliance to a standard had become overbearing. The increased call to overspecialization was causing us to become myopic, self-absorbed and somewhat indifferent to balance, harmony and care for others.

My new residence was a small, very old cottage on the rocky beach on the southeastern tip of Acadia National Park. It gave me access to a ferry boat ride to Nova Scotia and various locations along the Canadian coast. These were wonderful re-creative short getaways. I loved the pristine beauty of the untarnished lands in both areas. The air was clean. The wind bold yet friendly, even in the harshness of NE United States weather patterns. And, there was the spectacular antics of the Atlantic Ocean.

I was not a hunter of predatory fashion. My 35mm camera was put to good use in pursuit of various plant, animal and solid terrain encounters. I learned to develop my own photographs, most of which were black and white. This practice altered my perspective significantly in that it promoted a "self-do" attitude. The development of new skills necessary to complete the task followed soon thereafter. The most notable was patience and circumspection reaching levels not previously attained. Educators and Therapeutic Psychologists were much less patient and circumspect. At least this was so in my case.

The purchase of an old telescope brought me interaction with the night skies and its wondrous spectacles. The ongoing blanket of darkness surrounding my cottage was ideal for exploring the above and beyond. I could be a miniature Carl Sagan anytime I chose to. The constellations became alive as did certain planets like Venus and Mars. Much was learned about the self while pondering the stars. The endless array of the lights provided much thought and endless wonder. My schedule prompted early strolls along the beach, mid-morning to mid-afternoon writing, which occasionally carried into night fall. Then came the vista gazing the pearls of the sky which reinforced the beauty, peace and harmony of these nightly adventures. I began to realize that this was mentoring by the upper levels of the universe. It was quite obvious that I was becoming a universal citizen, a non-card-carrying member of this amazing partnership.

I was amazed at all times. This nightly ritual inspired more wonder, curiosity and awe. There never was a need for church, because the nightly venture brought humility, compassion and enormous gratitude for being allowed to experience this spectacle.It helped me to live right and function out of my truest center without serious need or want. It was here on a sand and water base that I found contentment. The evening vista coupled with an altered viewpoint fueled my source.

All was well!

It was here in this oceanscape that sailing came back into my life. Jacob, an old fisherman, who became my friend, taught me the value of the wind and the basics of sailing a small vessel in open waters. This "old salt", as he referred to himself, was tough as hickory, lived without medical aid and loved the sea and its many teachings. He was jovial but serious about life. He possessed and expressed profound wisdom in his life. A replant from Boston, he lived in this region since he abandoned city life and to some extent civilized patterns in general. Jacob was simple, honest and looked you in the eye at all times. He seldom criticized, was an avid conversationalist without drama and trivia. Actually, insignificant facts were avoided. He was an excellent story teller, especially when the story involved his personal experience of, with, or in the waters of the majestic Atlantic. This was his world. There was no other for him since he never left the New England coast. The Pacific Ocean was simply a bigger brother to the Atlantic, but in no way better. He heard about other oceans, but for Jacob, none matched the diversity and excitement of the Atlantic. For him the Atlantic was friend and constant companion whether Jacob sailed a vessel or walked its shore. The Atlantic Ocean was both his home and mentor.

His simple, honest demeanor camouflaged the fact that he had been a lawyer in the Massachusetts court system. He performed as a defense attorney with significant success. On occasion he spoke convincingly about political corruption and the injustice of our system of justice. No doubt this awareness deeply influenced his decision to remove self from it as well as the culture that tolerated such. For Jacob, social conflict stemmed from societal imbalance. The political and judicial systems created much disenchantment. Upon recognizing that the situation was unbearable, he decided to leave it rather than join it.

We spent much time on the open waters, endured some nasty storms but most ventures were in the good graces of fine weather. These were marked by benign steady winds and brilliant sunshine. More often than not, we sailed (sometimes for days) due east then north in order to avoid the shipping lanes and the large vessels that toted the want/need items of the American and Canadian people.

Our many trips revealed Hemingway's "Old Man of the Sea" image to me, personified and manifest in Jacob. His face, deep suntanned skin, brazen as leather, flexible as the wind with a profound penetrating, yet soft gaze reflected the history of a life at sea. Free from presumption, one guided by integrity, which always presented itself as a wholeness—one that was complete and fulfilled without complaint nor request for help. He was autonomous without being aloof, reliable without exception and always engaged in the wonder of consciousness. Life to Jacob was special and to be lived as sacred with compassion, humility and gratitude. His world was as wondrous as it was simple. To me it was appealing and highly desirable. However, there was a catch. To live such a life called for surrender of superficial wants and needs, and the endless attachments of western culture, American style. It was the culture of affluence, social-status-consciousness, and love of luxury. Jacob turned away from this cultural drone. He achieved his desire to free self from the "must have" in order to be happy. Without the "must-haves" no one could be satisfied or successful, so believed many who remained in the land he abandoned.

The refusal to continue on in conventional patterns was not a sudden desire. It was in the making for a long time. The dissatisfaction with the American dual standard, the injustice, and severe economic restrictions were in his mind and heart while in college and law school. These convictions and desire to be free of the inequalities increased, became clearer and drove the decision to make a change. As Jacob would say "I was there. I amassed the power, prestige, status, and vigorous capacity to earn more, gain influence, reach prominence and have numerous affiliations which rendered me fatigued, sapped my energy and prevented a normal, natural life style. I was distracted and somewhat inept."

He continued while gazing knowingly and innocently into my eyes, "that life style drained my substance, sapped my energy and prevented me from being more involved with nature's unfettered flow. I had become a player, a pawn in manipulative hands. I was on the fast track away from self and eager involvements with the true joys of life. My awakening opened a doorway to a new path. It was an intriguing path to follow in pursuit of the repossession of myself. My wants and interests were clarified. It took much time, effort, patience and an unrelenting perseverance."

When asked why there was such demanding requirements for a free-choice life, he was quick to respond: "the sea is easy to befriend, to revere its beauty and power. It is somewhat more difficult to function effectively with the ocean's rapid change, indifference to your situation, level of preparedness, or the ability to work (join) with it.

This is especially true during unforeseen or not previously experienced antics. There was always the need to surrender to its majesty and abundance in giving. The ocean is the ocean, always true to its ways. It is honest and ever ready to offer challenge as well as its bounty." He continued after clearing his throat, "I learned that to live in harmony with these waters, I had to join in oneness with the sea, to move with it, respect its fluctuations and always accept outcomes it delivered. I recognized the genuine symbiosis and eventually reveled in the shared splendor. Unfortunately, my wife and two adult children did not share my vision, nor my decision to make such a major transition."

I knew, in time, that I too was in the process of becoming a myopic "old salt" of sorts, thanks to Jacob and my willingness to avoid the bright lights and sound of civilized standards. I learned to awaken at dawn and retire at dusk. I also learned to live with the sea and survive by its bounty.

Refrigeration was the first to be released, followed by electricity, a standard stove, and all unnecessary auxiliary accommodations. My life had been distilled to the point of pure simplicity. My thoughts became clearer, as were my decisions. I chose candle light and small wood burner for heat and cooking. Wood scavenged from sea and shore became the frame for garden flowers and some vegetables like cucumbers, carrots, lettuce, onions, garlic, and zucchini. Tomatoes and potatoes grew well. So too, with the small raspberry patch. Some store purchases were necessary. Nevertheless, I was nearing a self-sufficient pattern. And, I liked it!

The persistence of my memory was my only contact with the past. Infrequent were recalls of teaching experiences. Less regular were retrievals of therapeutic engagements.

There was an exception to this, however. This was the warm, joy-filled time with Jennifer. The love we shared would never be lost to the past.

My time had come. My veins and brain were now directed by the sea and its salt.

FROM PINHOLE TO BIRDSEYE VIEW

My writing took a turn after two years of penning mementos and self-insights. I began to remember Keats and Shelly, Wordsworth and Dylan Thomas, Frost and other poets previously studied. I enjoyed and was moved by their command of the language. Their shared reverence for life continued to move me. I was entranced at times by reading and reciting their varied arrangements of nouns and verbs, intermixed with adjectives and adverbs. The experience was a joy revisited.

This reunion spawned my periodic feelings and experienced finding their way into my writing poetry. A word or thought or phrase thrust my very core into producing a flow of words, images and feelings. There was magic to writing like this. At times words came to me while at sea, strolling along the beach or deeply involved in the vastness of the brilliant sky. I would quickly jot down a line or sentence or a word or two before they were forgotten. At other times, an entire poem was completed in a few minutes. Some were rough drafts; some needed no rework. I wrote about darkness with no need for light, rain, walking, sharing, the open sea, the moon, love, freedom and numerous other topics. Other poems focused on Native American lands, the uncluttered self, the unfettered moment, the desire for and beauty of light, and stars call me to return. At all times there was an undeclared purpose, a sense of duty and service to the unknown value, the unidentified principle or source of absolute truth. It was working with freedom, yet words were guided by an unseen yet deeply felt force of persuasion and inspiration. At times I fantasized about being with such notables as Gandhi, Muir and F.L. Wright. Buckminster Fuller was there as well.

This new adventure grew into a passion which found a place within a cluster of driven-ness. The continuous prompt, the ever-present tug and the unending path forward, is what I called it—or them. At times it was like being pulled through/over water when sailing a small craft. On other occasions it resembled the push of an outboard motor. A tow and thrust experience, indeed. Either way it produced a trance-like moment that could be extended and extended.

I developed my own style. It always followed a free flow pattern. E.E. Cummings was always present in my poems as were Frost, Coleridge, and Wordsworth. Each of their presence had significant impact on my writing.

As time unfolded, I became keenly aware that my life had become simpler with less dependence on things. It had fused with nature. I slowly but continuously became more attuned to nature and its wondrous manifestation. My life was united with the harmony of my body, a prime unfolding of nature. It was immersed in the grand balance of all things. I was a part in the colossal scheme of that which we call consciousness. To be, or exist was to be an aware, sensate existence without the complications of societal hierarchies and positions of status and prominence. I now saw these as self-absorbed endeavors.

Consciousness was now understood and respected with increased reverence and gratitude for the ability to know, recall, observe, wonder, be awed and excited. The remarkable experience of being alive was surrounded by a cluster of astonishing activities and capacities. Prime to this union was the willingness to surrender oneself to another person. To love was essential to higher forms of consciousness. With love came compassion, kindness and wisdom, honesty and a host of positive social traits.

Jacob and I frequently conversed while on the water in the cool of calm evenings. A "There is too much logic and not enough care" Jacob would say. I agreed that the western world, if not all industrialized nations, were caught in the web of this skewed pattern. It involved a process marked by learn, apply to established patterns and get as much as you can in the material driven culture. The focus centered on attention on the self and continuous satisfaction of that self, wants and needs without end. It was a self-involved movement in history. As the conversation continued, both of us were quick to reaffirm that we had abandoned this tangle. We each at different times and through varied paths found our way to a fresher, more natural and interactive life style.

It occurred to me one clear sky evening that the ocean, sky and the simple life had replaced a previous life centered on power, status and prestige. It was a transition similar to the birth process. In the experience of escape from powerful influences, personal habits and incongruent preferences, celibacy was embraced whether by circumstance or choice remains open to debate. The respite from interpersonal heterosexual encounters suddenly became an issue of import for me. Yes, I had a good friend in Jacob. My numerous contacts with people on shore were enjoyable and supportive to my quest. However, there was no sexual other. No one to love in the fullest expression of this capacity that existed for me. A longing for female companionship increased in strength and frequency. I frequently asked myself who that person might be. There were no candidates in my limited commerce with others on land.

There was of course, attractive tourists who boated by, and other people who peered down on my humble setting from various shore points. I typically was more interested in mending a fish net or prepping food for a meal. No off-on relationship with tourist females for me.

I was older now. My libidinal drive had quieted some without expiring. There was tissue, cell and muscle memory and mindful desire. On occasion over the years I attended certain friend's family parties and celebrations. My presence was friendly, social and most courteous. There was little or no follow ups. Memories of past engagement with women flooded my brain and fueled desire for a woman. Who? How? Where? When? These were major questions to address for a man living the gift of life in a solitary manner. I knew it would come. It was on its way. Romance would return to me somehow.

Winter came quickly to Acadia. Wood, food supplies and securing the dwelling were done with haste. Winter season continued in modified fashion. The unpredictable Atlantic and usage of a small vessel breeds prudence. In a past summer I arranged an agreement with park officials for usage of the cottage. Since the tiny building had been taken off the seller's market, I was permitted squatters right to the location. My responsibility was to care for the place, not contaminate the area and do no harm to native animals. The park owed me nothing in return. Under the agreement I could stay as long as I choose to. Jacob had made a similar agreement years prior to my arrival. Unlike me he had a small permit tax and an obligation to pay for an over-catch fee. Actually, he infrequently brought in more fish than he needed to sell in order to survive and maintain the agreement.

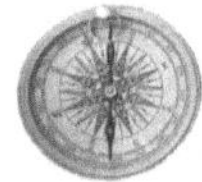

SWIRL (DAY OF)

Bald eagles, seahawks, and seagulls were plentiful at certain times of year. They felt free to help themselves to fish and other foods in the sun-dry process. We never chased them except when they became greedy and were given to gluttony and waste. Amazing creatures as they are, they can be pesky and very much aware of habit. One wonders about their sense of timing and arrival at prosperous moments. A seagull named Sparky would glide by and upon noticing the goodies on display, ignite the curiosity of the entire troop. No doubt, all partook of the available servings.

Certain unity among these feathered neighbors evolved eye-to-eye sort of. I pretty much knew when they were coming, and they sensed when tolerance prevailed. The typical squabbles over choice pieces were regularly observed. These noisy exchanges regularly alerted other fowl who then eagerly joined the episodic event. Eagles included.

All in all, these predators and scavengers were like friends. And friends always teach us important stuff.

Storms approached, fish running off shore, predators in the area. Dark, doom-oriented clouds dominated us and promised some rough times ahead. The wind came, the ocean heaved and the earth quivered in the face of the massive onslaught. It was a sight to behold as we hunkered down together for a long ride, directed by the storm. Well-rehearsed winds confirmed the onslaught as it embedded itself deep within our memory and rattled our door. There was good reason to believe that the high tide was going to do some serious damage. No matter what the meteorologists barked out in favor of minimal outcomes of the raging storm, we prepared for the worst. Window shutters were secured, debris was cleared, and the outdoor table, chairs and fish-prep station were cleared away. Nothing was left on the beach that could be transformed in an identifiable flying object of destruction. Our pace was hurried and focused on safety for us and those on the shore behind my dwelling.

As the storm intensified, we braced to ride it out. I had, prior to the clearing of beach and cottage items, secured my trusty sailboat in the hope it would escape serious damage. Food supply was ample as was kindling and fire wood. The meteorologists tooted a mini nor'easter but an inner voice cautioned us against underestimating the unfolding storm.

The storm spanned a seventy-two-hour period. It was coming in a most foreboding way as the headwaters tore into the beach.

Acadia knows heavy wind and ornery seas with knock out waves and dramatic surges. This storm tumbled out of a quick temperature change and a closely watched low pressure zone gathering force as they found unity. It revealed enormous momentum and a zealous confidence to have its way with this rocky shore. Once begun, as a light drizzle the rain continued with torrential force, heavy gales and amazing deluge. From a small window I was unable to distinguish shoreline from the water-surround.

The restless pounding on the roof turned deafening and remained in command of our focused attention. It was an orchestration of base drums, coupled with brass percussion in trumpeted blare. We attempted to sing loudly but were outdone by the relentless beating. Nothing dimmed the oppressive din. Sometimes a yell helped, momentarily. However, we eventually decided to attune our minds to it and become one with it. There was no choice. Conversation efforts were nothing more than lip movement and animated body/hand gestures. It was a siege. We huddled together and hunkered down for the remainder of this bizarre onslaught. It would end but in the moment of this surrealistic tangle we could only wait, help each other to survive, and live to tell about it. The experience was awesome, marked by danger accented in the present moment. In fact, it was surrealistic in its deep probe into our minds, souls and physical status. One could only surrender to the storms unfolding of power. Its gnash engulfed us, absorbed the territory and unleashed its repertoire. A multifaceted display of lightning, deafening thunder and relentless pounding rain revisited us, encore after encore.

When Spring finally turned things around, we spent time every day cleaning beach debris and salvaging wood cast up in winter storms and the unsettled Atlantic. We sorted wood into separate piles. Most of it ended up on the fire heap but select shapes were set aside for future furniture, shelves or for our simple fence. The experience typically tended to be fun-oriented. Imagination went wild and jokes flowed freely.

Nancy and I had weathered a Maine shore winter. Long hours indoors, limited sun and what at times were marked by endless boredom. Guitar strum tones kept us entertained. My battery driven Peerless 5 band radio was a welcome escape from the heavy storms and bitter cold, damp air temperatures. Strolls along the beach between 10:00 AM and 2:00 PM were also a respite from the winter blahs, the sun being a most welcome co-traveler. And, of course, the wind cleansed the soul and healed the body.

It was a memorable winter with below average snow fall on this island shore. The food supply held up and we were, with few exceptions, able to make it inland for our water supply. We used 10 to 15 gallons at a time for drink and cooking, the rest came from rain and snow salvage processed through a rudimentary filtration system. Nevertheless, the salt laced air frequently deposited its cargo into our water supply.

Most memorable were the warm fireplace times when we conversed about favorite movies, Broadway plays and various documentaries we had previously watched on T.V.

The blustery winds blew, waves rolled, currents churned, and Earth did its daily rotations. We were a semi-independent unit, Nancy and I. Laughter drove us beyond daily aches of aging bodies. We made exceptional effort to stay free from the chronic complaint and negative venue. And to no surprise, we succeeded. Habit became entrenched, thanks to the hippocampus and amygdala. What more could we ask for.? Survival needs satisfied (thank you Abraham Maslow!) and contentment prevailed. We willingly participated in discourse about death, meaning in life and purpose. Nancy incorporated Native American health advice, especially the Cherokee questions: who are we, why are we here and what is our purpose. She was fond of Cherokee medicine men/women stories. We, likewise, practiced self-healing and sharpened awareness, honed-in meditation to enhance togetherness and belonging. This life pattern rapidly moved into a ritual like tilt toward a fuller experience of life's offerings. We daily chose "to be over" the "not to be". It was a continuous decision to move forward and grow rather than stand still and/or regress in retreat from challenges inherent within the life encounter. A slowed down memory continued to be heralded over total loss of this wonderful capacity to remember. Rave on Buddy Holly! His music genius remains. But he is gone.

As is frequently the case, clean up after the storm is both an emotional and painfully slow process. Jacob stopped by to check out the condition of my property. After he greeted us and was satisfied that we were safe, he laughed, his eyes betrayed his deepest feeling, and said "C'est la vie." We sat in the debris cluttered beach and had food from my pantry. We shared some fresh coffee and cheerful bantering. The winds had come and gone, the ocean waters, however, continued their tyranny, clouds wept periodically, and the earth quivered in response. Boats in the harbor bobbed and slid like yo-yos doing ballet. It was a site to remember as Nancy uttered an excited "Wow! What power!"

Nancy had met Jacob a few weeks back shortly after arriving from Springfield, MA where she taught Native Cultures at Holyoke Community College. They took to each other as if they knew each other for many, many years. They tested each other's wit, laughed effortlessly and challenged and amended thoughts and topics discussed. An immediate friendship unfolded. She had asked to visit me once she learned I was living in Acadia. It was an unexpected request since we had little contact following the divorce years ago. I detected an unspoken need in her request to come and talk with me. I agreed, told her she was welcome and prepared for her arrival.

My mind, puzzled at her desire to share some time together, then shifted focus to my choice to help in whatever way I possibly could. I recognized that I never lost my feelings for her. I might easily say that there remained a soft, warm spot for her in my heart. However, I entertained thoughts centered on what her needs were and a haunting question on whether I was capable of dealing with the emotional onslaught of spending time together once more. There was bound to be a truck full of emotional baggage.

Nancy retained her beautiful presence in the world. She was slim and retained her well-distributed assets. She continued turning heads in her direction. The daughter of an Irish-immigrant doctor, she grew up in the Midwest and earned a B.A. and M.A. in Anthropology at Michigan University and Chicago University respectively. Notable credentials included significant studies in the Amazon Rain Forest, some discoveries in the sands of Egypt, and the most distinguished involvement, searching the pueblos in New Mexico at Chaco Canyon, and in Colorado near Mesa Verde. She had, what I call, a gentle intellect, always willing to share insights, its capacities and brilliant holdings. As such, she was not aggressive or intent on impressing others. If anything, she unfolded a calming effect in conversations with others. A keen and very appropriate humor accompanied her other personal gifts. Some people said she brought calm and laughter with every step she took.

IF CIRCLES COULD TALK

Awakening in pre-dawn, the lark having done its daily chore, I was ready once again, as the sun spun up out of the horizon, to make several life-changing decisions. Nancy and I reconnected, reawakened the chemistry and renewed our entwinement. We, in a short time, recreated, or simply acknowledged an unbroken oneness. It proved to be a unity that had been fractured some but not severed. The passage of time did not erase the magnetic attraction we experienced and relished. She was more beautiful than ever. Her radiant smile had become more attractive and most assuring to all who received it. In all, she was confident in a different way. It was less intimidating, more mature and in no way did it suggest superiority. The confidence she exuded was genuine, warm and revealed a person at peace with herself. Obviously, she was easy to be with.

This recent reconnect emerged out of more than chemical tug. It was a reconciliation marked by forgiveness for past offenses and abuses of matrimonial commitment. It was real and both of us knew it. There was no denying that we enjoyed being together again. Laughter and well-known game play on each other were common in and around the cottage. Somehow, surviving the storm together proved cathartic. We, within the assault of the storm were awakened to awareness that we still cared deeply for each other. What at one time had been a professional-laced relationship directed by strict societal guidelines under the tutelage of extreme religious values, the relationship now was lighter, freer-spirited with more spontaneity and reduced seriousness. Fun was pivotal, as was an ever-present sense of awe in mutual gratitude for the reunion. Consequences of stress were minimized by the playfulness of our togetherness.

We were happy, at peace with the relationship and partnered in a common vision of future moments. We knew where we were going. And we definitely were aware of where we had been. Nancy and I celebrated this renewed joy with frequent silent embraces and regular positive comment on our new-found and clearly different from past experiences. Silent, prolonged gazing into each other's eyes ratified the fact that we were in love again. Who was the thinker who noted "all is well that ends well?" If someone had observed our earlier relationship, separation and reunion, one might easily have judged and explained what in fact "goes round, comes around…" and as Teilhard de Chardin asserted "all that rises must converge." And so it goes.

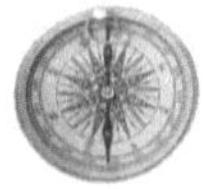

Cobble It Down: The Past as Reflected in the Future

Nancy, as high tide tumbled in stride with our pace upon the beach, said "Matt, we should not look back. We have a new identity and a history to create. We are who we are, different than years past and yet similarity remains. Our personal experience is different as is our willingness to remain open to what is possible. Both of us are admirers of Albert Camus and the existential life style which is driven by freedom and the ceaseless call to personal responsibility for one's behavior. The fear that drives people to conformity has no impact on you and me. We are unique in our individuality, what we do as conscientious decision makers. There is little in our lives to comply with."

She paused briefly, reset her tone which had wavered toward the end of her passionate assertion. Emotions and feelings returned to normal mode as she slowed her walk, looked at me with deep intensity while uttering in clear voice that matched her eye:

"I'm glad that I wanted to see you again after so many years. And I am joyous that you invited me to visit"

My response welled up from deep within my core surrounded by a warm full smile:

"This is a special moment. I want more of this. More and more of you and me together. Please stay as long as you wish. In fact, why not move in permanently. As we've seen recently, there is plenty of room in the cottage." The pause that followed might have lasted 2 seconds or several minutes as we peered into each other's' eyes. What followed was a mutual declaration of our re-cemented love.

Destiny or openness or perhaps unconscious desire had reunited us. We were once again a pair, a couple, a oneness of sorts. There was no need to analyze it. I just wanted to bask in the beauty of the moment.

Our life from that particular stroll along the beach marked a new beginning of what once had been a young marriage turned sour. This seaside relationship without want of contract had similar glue but more adhesive grip to it. We once more grasped happiness laced with a clearer lens, untarnished, sweeter taste to it. Like a well-cared for bee hive's honey, we merged, blended and filtered our way to a trance like but most delectable nectar. Indeed! We ditched politics, religion and medicine. We lived by the light of the sun and the flame of the fire wood and candle. We delved more deeply into the sky above and the sea below. We walked and walked and talked endlessly about our perceptions, illusions, beliefs and hopes as well as our growing gratitude for life and the sheer joy of living this mystery. Periodically we pondered the world's lunge toward insanity with needless war, increased levels of poverty and hunger, growing greed, economic disparity and the promise of environmental decline. Our concern for tens of thousands of daily child deaths around the world from preventable disease and massive malnutrition occupied our minds especially when the numbers released by UNICEF turned alarming. Considering our limited capability, we absorbed the reality in a compassionate manner and reinforced our decision to live an independent, simple, yet cooperative life with our planet.

In response to this rapid change of the world's pace, we waited, thought and prayed to God as mystery, the universe, and perhaps to the collective unconscious to open up paths to solution for the increased world problems. It had become obvious that Democracy, Capitalism, Free Market, Socialism, Communism and Dictatorial schemas continued to fail the needs of nations and the globe in general. A broader, simpler ideology was needed. The world needed an ideology that shoe-horned a life commitment that pivoted on right relationship with other humans, animals, the world and all situations that occurred. Some call this justice.

Nancy and I focused on care and kindness as the new model. Society as we know it would not survive. This steady erosion of society and planet stability, would not, in any way support an identification of universal citizenship. Nevertheless, the unfolding of each future moment bolstered the hope of a much better world. A world marked by global good, not simply prosperity for those nations with economic, military and science/technology superiority. In the meantime, we would build our connectedness on this plot of land called Mount Desert Island.

ON LOOKING BACK

The world divides us. In fact, it fractures us and causes pain and many problems. The life within the world heals and mends us. Life is the salve. It soothes and exhorts beyond the nicks, bumps, bangs and knocks. The core of life, the heart, is in charge of the remedy process we call healing. It is good, golden and an endless giver. The pump, as it were, also senses the genuine and true need. It monitors all that passes through its chambers and recognizes the good, the bad and tolerates the ugly. This ultimate organ is the pulse beat of our existence and perhaps the universe.

As Nancy and I agree, the heart shapes behavior and mends broken fences. It carries to us the necessary hope and aspirations to chase goals, endure trauma, declare choice and maintain balance. However, as Nancy reminds me: "The heart bows in the presence of the mind. Brain is prince. Mind is king." And when I think of it, mind-over-matter continues to reign. There is no consciousness without mind. This I believe. In fact, this I know.

Consciousness is the kernel of life, the source of all that is. No clear explanation, I simply state my simple non-scientific judgment as a behavioral psychologist turned Naturalist—perhaps Pantheist. All that I know and currently focus my life on is tied to my union with Nature. Stars, clouds, sun-moon, sea and spray, sand, gravel and the changing wind captured my attention and imagination, then swept me from the world of the #1's and top canines to a neutral, fair, honest and even-leveled existence. This world of harmony in which living creatures thrive, find peace and co-operation in a unified, shared and responsible manner. Thank you Jacob, Wendell Berry, John Muir and so many other mindful people. I need to find a way to raise nuts and harvest seeds in and from a sandy soil. I am more and more aware of other mindful people.

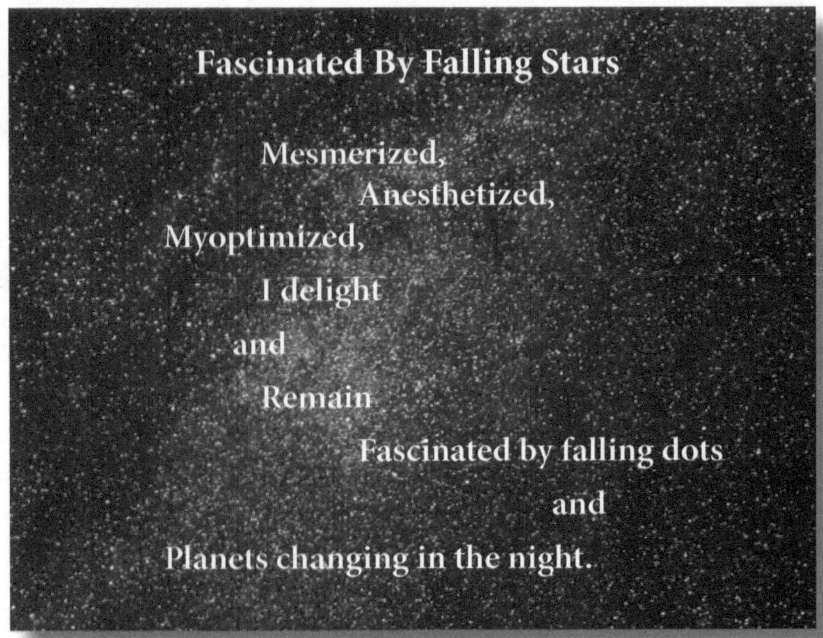

For now, I will deepen my union with nature, do no harm and limit waste. This is a 180-degree swing from my Pittsburg ways.

Today, I am more concerned about preservation and the continuation of simplifying my/our own life. The earth spins, the stars shine, the sun and moon come and go. I breathe, feel, think, know and remember. I try to think less and feel more, eat less but increase my activity, breathe deep and slow. I try to talk less and listen more as I relearn the value of kindness (mostly from Nancy) in acts both great and small. No easy task. Not like knowing or memorizing a truth or fact and answering questions on an academic exam or simply teaching someone to do a particular something or action, thought, feeling and so on. No! To be kind to others calls for a galvanized conviction about being and behaving as a person of kindness. Seeing it as good and choosing to do from a habit of being kind in all situations. Someone has said "kindness is the measure of a man." Knowledge is secondary to doing. Action needs to follow conviction.

The simple life has helped me to be strong, healthy and whole (complete). I am more free than I was prior to settling in Maine. Financial concerns are minimal. Living expenses were greatly reduced. The decision to cancel electrical, water and gas services was an instrumental factor to the simplification process. I recall a recent conversation in which Nancy said "upon learning of your move to a simpler life and seeing first hand just how you lived, I said, 'nice move sailor'. I marveled at the ease with which you were able to rid self of unnecessary burdens. I find it somewhat puzzling how a man like you managed to radically simplify your life and continue to enjoy it."

"Why?"

"Because you attained a level of prominence as a professor at a highly successful university. You enjoyed the good life with all of its gusto. In fact, this transition was not something I foresaw on the horizon. No need to tell you how much I admire you for doing it." Her eyes were round and full as she bent forward to enhance her conviction.

"I heard it from a mutual friend that you disengaged from the university, but I needed to see it myself. It's the investigator in me."

"Is that why you asked me if you could visit and check it out?"

"Yes, indeed. If you were not involved with someone and were open to my request…why not. I was eager to the venture."

"Pity the clock."

"Good observation," she replied.

"So where do we go from here?"

The vivid memory continued to manifest in my head. "Let's see where second chances lead."

She paused slightly, then, with a slow deliberate tone said: Matt, I forgive you and me for past infractions and selfish behavior. You appear to be of similar mind. Is this not so? If not, simply let me know and I will be on my way. I do, however, have this vision of and for us. It in no way resembles the Hollywood overuse of the lost then renewed relationship prancing off into the sunset."

Indicating my openness to the possibility of a second run at a successful relationship, I gently nodded and in a drawn out low voice said, "so…"

Laughter, perhaps more a nervous relieved giggle and mild tears interlocked in the moment.

"This vision carries a central practice of testing the waters. No looking back stuff. No churning up old wounds, emotional scars and painful memories. It was clearly focused on the present moment and the exchange of two human beings who found love earlier in their life together. Could we once again be a 'one', a union of more seasoned adults cultivating a desirable harmony?" she asked.

Another pause and encouraging "and..."

"Well, simply put, I said yes to it. No scientific study or analysis, thank you. A basic

'let's try it' will be enough for me."

"I agree to do it. Not simply try it. I remember our early years. Fun, laughter and good times! Always!"

And that was that.

Nancy resigned from her employment post and shortly, thereafter, donated unwanted possessions to the Salvation Army. She stored other things and journeyed north to Mount Desert Island to be with me. Journeys begin with a first step and Nancy took that step. The journey moved forward toward a common vision rooted in desire and need. But I analyze here. The story board reflected an honest effort on our part. In the end, if our intent were to hold fast, our life together would be markedly different than our first rendezvous.

And so, it has been an ongoing togetherness.

ANOTHER SPRING DAWNS

When it was done and the deep afternoon relished extended sun, Nancy and I began to work our way out of the winter dullness. Wayward driftwood with no direction home were gathered and added to our ever-heightened wood piles. The rock infested beach lost sand and topsoil to periodic storms. Several truckloads of soil brought in from the mainland to create a vegetable /fruit garden served me well. This year's past winter repairs included replacing the kidnapped soil. Erosion was a continuous challenge to my non-engineer background.

The Saab 96 trunk toted buckets of soil to the shore. The National Park authorities permitted ten 5 gallon buckets each Spring as needed. The mix of sand and careful blend of top soil created a nourishing bed for varied seed to flourish. The Fall-Winter compost worked wonders as well.

In addition to readying the garden, there remained roof mending, securing shingles and removal of meddlesome rock and stone. All in all, the winter was after all, do-able, if not somewhat easy on us. There was less snow than previous years, a bit higher temperature range, more sunshine and less cloud cover (according to meteorologists). The winter blahs quickly faded as they yielded to the promise of springtime. To our west trees showed buds awaiting the call to blossom and decorate the landscape with thousands of unique hues or shades of greenness. Monet and Van Gogh would revel in delight of such a shore-scape site. What marvelous vistas cast upon the senses in wonder laced with awe and welcomed embrace. When one is immersed in nature's seasonal manifestation, there is only wonder and reverence about and to the

Spring Equinox. There was also the task of relocating my sailboat, the Quicksilver, from its winter hibernation in a nearby harbor. Dragged, with the help of a makeshift trailer to the water's edge, rudder and sails were fixed as the vessel was readied for the sea. We slowly motored our way to the area in front of the cottage and anchored her.

The next day, the Spring tides steadied themselves and warm temperatures called me to open waters and the unmatched winds of the Atlantic. A first day back into the salt brought muscle memory and brain functions into a renewed and enjoyable reactivation.

Sailing was fun and an ever-present challenge. One needed to read the wind, recognize waves as friend or foe and not fall prey to bravado, but become one with the sea and what it was willing to offer at any given moment. It clearly demonstrated that you cannot capture the ocean, let alone the wind. You can only join it in adventure.

Once out into open water I suddenly realized that the wind, water, saiboat and I once again, were one. We moved as one. We were one. I was the sail as it embraced the stiff steady wind. I was the wind urging the sail to expand and billow forth. I was the water accommodating the craft. I was each of these without distinction. They were me, I them, simultaneously. We were a single unit of swift movement in a specific direction. With my hair reshuffled and prancing continuously, water splashing up from the side, rudder knowing an unspoken destination but keenly aware of the vessel's intent, we effortlessly powered forward. My face was a compass, the winds provided persuasion, as the sea held us in Herculean fashion. We were flying or floating without deference to the laws of physics. We simply glided. I was not simply a man going for a ride, I was a force thrusting along a predestined path, a nautical line, an unmarked seaway. It was somehow Utopia, or at least in a very pleasant, pain free altered mental state—AUM....

While cruising at what appeared to be close to the speed of light, Jacob's advice found its way to the forefront of my brain: "You cannot conquer the sea, you can only be a part of it with respect, awe and enjoyment. She is mother to all. She is a contributor to the mystery of creation. Water connects all. From rain and snow come the rivulet, brook, stream, creek, lake and river. An unbroken cycle. All are interconnected with lakes, springs and ponds. These are the sources of life we call the verdant and breathing. These are the hidden waters." Bravo H2O!

When did the lunar sphere link up with the waters of the world? And what came first the cloud or the vapor? Perhaps it took place during a negative ion blitz that the moon found appealing. Shine on you luminary of the second class! We too share a connection and dream, so gleam on.

Additional Jacobian words of wisdom pivoted in my head and moved to the frontal lobe:

"An old sailor's rule is to never go to sea in a boat smaller than the seas you will encounter. Know what your vessel can handle. And remember, experience and know-how is a process continuously evolving"

Clouds darkened as a blustery wind ushered in a drop in temperature. High tide was intent on slamming the beach several miles west. The upper tier of the island beaconed out to sea for all sailors to take note. Not a call to be ignored, I chose to be no different than any careful sailor. I slowly slid the rudder to swing to a more north-easterly direction. The Quicksilver responded beautifully which told me we were still in unison.

The decision proved beneficial as the main sail cupped the strong steady wind. A wind that was both invigorating and clearly duty-bound. The surge of the shifting waves would not rank as a sailor's delight. However, the up, down pattern was enjoyable as the wind reminded memory and know-how in such situations. The bow continued, meeting wave surge at the proper angle while staying on course to shore. The clouds thickened as they moved from a fading grey-white to heavy grey-black spread out and flat pattern. Obvious indicators of heavy on-board power well known as thunder and lightning laced with pelting rain. Numbness ahead. Just what I needed for a first Spring run on the water.

The Quicksilver was sturdy and easily handled the pounding waters. I remained calm as we headed back to shore. With a swift wind in my sails, I was at the beach within minutes. I anchored the QS after sails were dropped and secured, rudder locked, then hopped aboard my trusty dingy. It was a worthwhile reacquaintance with the Atlantic via its entertaining mood. No sooner was I inside the door when a huge streak of lightening tore through the sky followed by a tumult of thunder and heavy rain. Nancy was starting a small fire to chase the dampness away. It was a great day for the landlubber for the rest of the day.

Voices of the Sea

Call of the water upon the rim.
Rolling thunder drumming shore
Thrashing waves bashing boats.

Echo rebound from heavy skies
Clouds laden in bold array
A whisper of "stay and play."

Flowing sound of harps;
Trumpeted blare amidst storms of delight mixed with fright,
O, how I love voices of the sea.

Partnered melody with wind,
Swept to new locals and deeper tones
Gentle ballad in sunscape days
Open sea music to the ear

Soft winter hymns in snow squall times
Listen to the roar, murmur and sigh
As horizon blends to sky.

The splash upon sail and mast reminds of symphonies heard
from the past.
Flute tones calm troubled spirit,
Roused by vigorous percussion, with melodious strings
And pleasant sounds abound.

None like those upon earths ground.
Awakened soul by voices of the sea,
That's where this sound tend be.

Blue-gray waters ranging free
No rage in open sea.
Every gesture of sound, a response to sky, sun,
Wind and moon's continued look.

Churn, churn the tide of sounds
Using varied call to invite
Willing sailors to ongoing delight.

Wind swept refrain before rain
Is never the same nor from similar setting,
Was it the cloud or the water that came first?

Calm the spirit
Quell fear

Bid personal presence to belonging and oneness

Utterance of the sea be
Many to ear that listen
And follow the call of mist-laced voice
Revealing secrets in whisper and shout

Watch out! We're coming about!

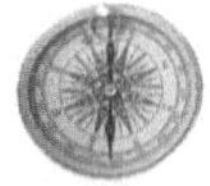

D.G. Esposito

TIME TICKS SLOWLY WHEN YOU'VE LOST LOVE

I've never heard from Jennifer since we parted. Common friends with whom I've retained periodic contact report she is well and living in southern Florida. She's not married and is more deeply committed to her craft. Apparently, she continues her love affair with traveling the globe and never tires of encountering the varied peoples and cultures. I continue to wish her well and truly miss her at times. As the ancient writers assert: "It is better to have loved and lost than to never have loved at all." As well, I am forever reminded of Einstein's recommendation, "Learn from yesterday, live for today, hope for tomorrow."

I was captivated by sailing at an early age. An uncle was my teacher, so, upon telling him of my interest, we were off on weekends for sailing adventures at Lake Hopatcong and Budd Lake. Both lakes were within an hour's drive of Newark. Uncle Ken, my mother's brother learned to sail in the Navy and owned a small 14-foot craft which he kept at the Hopatcong Yacht Club. It was a simple vessel that I loved. Easy to handle, it swept up and down the 9 mile stretch of Hopatcong. I particularly liked the heavy winds that kicked up lumbering waves and white caps. These blustery blasts infected me with a love for sailing. There was the continuous excitement and wonder as well as the comforting swish as water gushed by and impacted the rudder. A soothing experience, yet difficult to put into words. As I reflect back, it began a meditative trance-like state of mind. Attentiveness to wind, weather, the swing of the boom when "coming round," and concern for other vessels was not lost in the particular involvement with direction and the free, unadulterated beauty of sailing. Wonder what it was like to be on a Viking boat, a Polynesian tub, Captain Ahab's "Pequot," or the Mayflower.

At times while sailing I fantasized about sailing my own craft (a yacht perhaps) to Cape Cod, or Long Island Sound via the Newark Bay by way of the Passaic River, then into Upper Bay through the East River and entering the Sound at the Throgs Neck Bridge. My most lavish dream centered on a slow sail along the coast to the Bahamas. I was to live there and explore the various islands. Bimini Island appealed to me for some reason or other.

As a sailor, Uncle Ken required me to learn nautical terms and the parts of a sailboat. Long but enjoyable hours of study at age 10 brought preparedness and astonishing wonder at the various names. The bow, deck, hull, keel, rudder, port and star board, sail (main and jib), mast, anchor, back stay, boom, halyard, leeward and wind ward direction became common lingo for me. As Jacob was fond of saying "…there is so much to learn and love about sailing." For him, sailing was a lifestyle, a specific way to spend your life.

Jacob and Uncle Ken would've been great friends if and when they had met. No chance of that happening. Uncle Ken died a few years ago at the hand of cancer. He was a man of many talents and possessed an open and a good heart. He earned his living as an electrical engineer at the RCA research in Morristown, NJ. He taught me well. By the time I was in high school my sailing skills were well groomed. I was eager to try out some of my dreams of ocean sailing. However, Rutgers University's call was loud and clear. No need to say I accepted the invitation to attend. I began my freshman year following high school graduation. A clear vision of a specific goal was not part of this college entry. I did recognize my knack for helping people sort-out situations and enable them to make constructive decisions. I began to see self as a developmentalist, a coach of sorts, for individuals grappling with personal difficulties. A source of objective and concise input capability surfaced early in that first year. Without knowing it, I was on a path to a psychology future. This evolving awareness prompted me to choose a Bachelor of Science track in Psychology with as many soft science electives as the curriculum allowed.

I was a day-hop student. This in-out involvement did not hamper my academic performance, nor severely limit social connections. A decision to side-step fraternity membership offers, but enthusiastically nod yes to private, personal invites from various gals in sorority life proved prosperous. The dances and parties were enjoyable and brought a steady flow of dates and beneficial relationships. Some girls were quasi steady for many years of on/off campus life. No need to touch upon them now. Suffice to say, all was good. Some relationships were better than others. A few were exceptional connects.

A 3.5 GPA accompanied me as I received my sheepskin. The event was uplifting and provided me with a unique sense of accomplishment and liberation. Mom and Dad seemed to simply float along during the entire ceremony and the family celebration following the formal rubrics. After all, yours truly was the first to complete a college degree. Do wonders ever cease?

Upon completion of a summer job at the Rutgers University Behavioral Care Center I prepared to depart for the University of Chicago. While pursuing an M.S. in Psychology I worked as a dormitory resident director plus some minor peer care tutoring involvements. The graduate school challenge, marked by much lab work, private research and numerous papers carefully evaluated by professors was at times daunting but doable. I enjoyed the expansion of knowledge which trickled into a larger world view both personal and collective. The New School of Psychology begun by Carl Jung was most intriguing as was the client-centered approach of Carl Rogers. I knew in the early stages of grad school that these two therapeutic practices would serve as my therapeutic base. Little did I realize at that time, however, that the therapeutic foundation was not pot-hole exempt, nor bump and knock down free. We learn as we go. We learn as well from, with and because of the people we encounter throughout life. We somehow remain connected. An unending varied connect in the astro-physical and general communication with or without personal contact, there exists a continuous unity of variable degrees of togetherness. The reign of the Universal Unconscious does not fail to impress nor influence our individual/collective life.

There were many relations during the two-year commitment at the University of Chicago. Many were fellow students trudging through the mechanics of a graduate degree in Psychology. Some were co-workers.

Others were mere acquaintances. There was an array of women as well. Some were lonely girls struggling to stay afloat in the complexities of the city life. There were the to-be-professional with eyes on Wall Street and large corporations like General Electric, Pittsburg Steel, and the automobile empires. Other women encountered (simply sex-casual connects) helped fill the social gratifications I harbored. No girl friend or long-term relationship for me. I was simply satisfying needs. No dangling emotions here. Simple, pointed and carefully regulated dating. These were upfront and straight forward. No damage or unnecessary scars. All were no-harm connects. A simple enjoyment between the dots of societal necessity. Several women shared many interests and compatible life style with mine. But my plan had clear relationship limits; none to be breached or ignored. The plan was a diligent pilot transporting me through this particular period of my life flight.

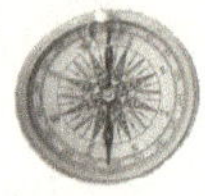

THEN CAME THE WOMAN

As I look back now about my road to Acadia, there appears to be a winding-like path of linkage and connections created mostly by choice but some by chance and or serendipity. I wonder about the difference between free choice and causal effect. I elect to allow the philosophers to figure that one out. However, synchronicity is a very strong magnet for a steel-minded will such as mine. Click! Click! Click! That enviable sound of magnetic poles in unpreventable mode we call connect. The unavoidable manifesting. Wow!

During my well-practiced dating strategy, a very strange and unexpected thing happened. Jim Becker, a fellow psych grad student asked me to attend an Anthropology presentation by a well-known Anthropologist. The core of the lecture (with slides) focused on yet to be discovered artifacts from various cultures hidden in sand and beneath modern-day dwellings. Jim had an interest in a particular Sociology major he met the day before in the U's library. She told him she would go for a drink with him if he met her at the presentation. So, there I was trying to stay interested in anthropological digs. I might better have stayed at the dorm and studied or listened to undergraduate drones. At that moment Gina said, "hey guys let's go for that drink."

On the way out, Gina paused to say hi to a fellow grad student. Her friend responded to Gina as she slowly turned and glanced into my eyes as we were introduced. The world stopped and then stuttered a bit as the glance whirled into a prolonged connect. It was Jim who fractured the magnificence of the moment, "well what's say we go have that drink." The three of us agreed to depart. But before the first step was taken, I came out with, "See you again, nice meeting you Nancy." I nearly did a cartwheel. It was an exhilarating initial junction. Untold number of emotions bathed my whole being. I saw a burst of miniature asterisk-like sparkles and I found myself to be nervous and wobbly. We all know the butterfly in the belly feeling.

I immediately wanted to know her more fully as I blurted out "Gina, nice meeting you." Followed by "I need to get to know Nancy. Do you know much about her? Is she involved with anyone? Please tell me if she asks about me. I need some time to myself. See you later. No! Here is my phone number. Let me know if you think she would go out with me. Enjoy your drink. Bye Jim, thanks for an enjoyable night."

I was entranced. I did not know how to handle this or keep things within the borders of my plan. Control abandoned me. I was at the mercy of fate.

Synchronicity was at work here. For the remainder of the evening I was swarmed with the continuous replay of our meeting. The next day was the same as were the days that followed. Studies were on temporary hold. There was nothing here but a man beginning to feel and partially know his future. This was new and most unusual as I discovered this awareness over and again. Nancy's face and glistening eyes were pad-locked in my brain.

No imaginings here. The vivid experience of being completely held by another's entwined glance carried its own focus. We simply had to meet again and again. The crystal-clear recall dominated both brain and body. I was mesmerized. Her face revealed all. She was beautiful with radiant, willing to engage eyes, high cheek bones, perky lips and an alert presence. Her physical assets were bountiful. Her glance was piercing but not offending or intrusive. It was the look that goes in, through and around you at one and the same moment. All that I know was that I wanted to be with her, to spend my life with her. She was the one to go through time with to paraphrase Jim Croce. Hands down. No question! She was the one, the girl for me.

When Nancy and I learned of each other's interest, thanks to some middle-man work by Jim and Gina, we began seeing each other. Both of us had busy schedules, but somehow squeezed out some free unin-terrupted time together. The mutual attraction coupled with a dizzying infatuation deepened the already profound ramifications of being smitten. No rational choice here. It was untainted out–of-controlness and we reveled in it. Love out maneuvered controlled plan.

This chance meeting took place three months prior to being graduated, Nancy in Anthropology and me in Psychology. The issue of where do we go from here moved to the center of our shared life. Both of us were accepted in doctoral programs in several universities. The issue took on a gut and mind twist type of perplexity in that we declared our love for each other and chose to stay together as best as possible without doing harm to career goals. The University of Chicago accepted both of us as candidates. Option #1 was to remain in Chicago, rent a dwelling, use the professional contacts we had in order to land part-time employment. Option #2: One of us could work while the other earned the door-opener degree. This option provided income to carry us to graduation. The doctoral candidate would help with part-time work. Option #3: Utilize the academic and earning opportunities that come with an individual's credentials backed by major degrees from a variety of institutions of higher learning. Welcome to the world Western Civilization trumpets: "the more clout, the further you go." Money to be made is the key to economic power and prestige. Option #4: Drop the doctoral pursuit. Get teaching jobs, marry, have kids and choose a location to set up shop.

We chose the first option. We completed our doctoral mandates for the prestigious degrees and were on our way. This decision worked to our advantage. Nancy did some teaching at the undergraduate level and assisted the faculty. I was able to work at both the University of Chicago's Mental Health Center in center city and was a part-time therapist at a counseling center. The combined income, with the help of student loans enabled us to cover living and educational costs.

The efficiency apartment, a small but furnished basement one, was pleasant and satisfied our needs. Class schedules were different as were work time involvements. Time together was limited but just enough to keep our love affair alive and well. The only thing that suffered was sleep. Each of us survived on minimum sleep without losing effectiveness as a student, a worker and as a spouse. Stress was abundant, but we managed to always be present to each other. However, as time whizzed by and the completion of our studies was near, we stumbled and hit an impenetrable wall. Shortly after we learned that we were to be parents in late summer, our joy was splintered by a mindless indiscretion on my part. The blunder took place at the private counseling center meeting in early December. The younger workers decided to have a few drinks at meetings end. To shorten a very long, painful and involved story, Nancy found out about my adulterous episode with a grad school woman who also worked at the center. To make matters worse, Nancy suffered a miscarriage in late February. Both events were devastating for her. She refused marriage counseling and opted out of the marriage. Upon receiving her doctorate, she accepted work that took her to Egypt. I was filled with guilt and grief. Heavy drinking followed more heavy drinking as my refusal to deal with problems continued. As pain accompanied my downward spiral I bolted west to the City of Angels. And yet, here I was, once again with Nancy. Oh, the winds of change!

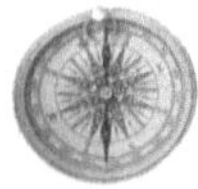

To the Sea Again

A paint brush sky was fellow traveler today as we ventured into open sea. My Pearson Triton sailboat had some wear and tear on it but cut through waves as designed back in 1959 at Portsmouth, Rhode Island. The Quicksilver was a fiberglass hull, slept four and was one of the affordable used crafts available in the general Maine area. I became aware of it through an old friend who had settled in Bar Harbor many years ago. He clued me in on its availability during a chance meeting while I was having a beer and some steamed clams in a bar. The price was just right for my pocket book. The boat had some heavy usage by a family in Kennebunkport. It came on market two years ago but remained free of any purchase bids. The price was reduced for this 1964 version since it showed some heavy scars from scrapes with pier docks and ocean debris. Some redo work and a good cleaning rendered it ready for the water. Apparently, the previous owner did not put any heavy wear on the outboard engine. So, I made a good deal. I now owned a 26-foot seaworthy vessel. A cruiser as it was classified.

The easterly flow of popcorn clouds and varied billow-shaped forms provided an added pleasant view. Nancy and I found many commonly identified patterns. The pace of cloud movement was slow and easy which allowed us to focus on the shapes and look-alikes. A clown, bear, and castle appeared early on followed by a tunnel, two gypsies running and one funnel cake. After a while, as we headed out to deeper waters "what an imagination" said Nancy.

"Well, I wasn't the one who saw gypsies," I replied.

"Yes, okay, but who was it that found a dancing bear?"

"Can I help it if I happen to like the animal? Besides, there is a need to stay on course," I retorted.

"Aha! Excuses! Excuses followed by excuses."

"Who me? Just being creative."

"Where are we headed anyway?" Nancy asked.

"It's a surprise."

Actually, Jacob earlier alerted me of a Blue Fish run two- or three-mile due east. Hours and hours of Blues just waiting to be taken. Last summer we were able to catch eight Blues as they ran just off shore beyond the breaking waves. We stood with bamboo poles and 15 to 20 feet of line while standing in water up to our waists. They swam while feeding several feet from the breaking waves. It was fun and very exciting to get a bite and firmly nurse it to a floating basket. Nancy got five to my three. Women dominate the world!

Suddenly Nancy called out "dolphins!" A school of dolphins were 200 yards from us weaving through the water heading south in pursuit of prey.

"Pity the prey. Dolphin swim patterns of movement reminded me of a tailors stitch in cloth, smooth and effortless."

"Yes. It is both beautiful and tragic. Both are aspects of a central part of nature's unfolding. Matt, have you ever wondered why we animals eat each other in order to survive? Perhaps there's no other way for the different species to carry on and evolve," Nancy mused.

"Well, if Buddha was correct in his assertion that what we think, do, feel and eat, we become, and we apply the belief, we are somehow the same. We are each other. One!"

"Wow! What insight and wisdom. Actually, little fish eat micro-organisms and algae. Larger fish eat the smaller and so on up the food chain. And in the most original and oldest recycle, dead animals and plants decompose, their respective nutrients then flow into streams, creeks, rivers and oceans of the world. This completes one cycle only to mark the beginning of another. It's a perfect system requiring no recalibration or repair. It is a natural flow. It was a continuous anticipation and usage of the ritualistic process." At that moment, a glance at the compass spoke clearly that we had veered off course. A simple slide of the rudder made it well again.

"There we go. Please continue," I urged.

"From the very beginning to this moment and beyond this set-up ensures survival of the diverse species. Quite a plan. Somehow random causal effect falls short of what this magnificence reflects. Perhaps we exist in an intelligent universe. Who knows?"

"Yes indeed!"

We sailed a bit before we spotted the endless school of Blues who were involved in a delectable delight, non-frenzied feast. Lines were cast and successful catches landed. There was no time to count who got what. A simple take what was needed. No over-catch. The sea's bounty has and will satisfy our needs. And besides, both Nancy and I

learned the value of "enough is enough" principle. As Gandhi put it: "take and use only what you need."

On the return to port we discussed the method of de-scaling, gutting and drying the delicious taste of the Blue Fish. We would, of course, charcoal the biggest catch of the day covered with fresh herbs from the garden. We no longer used retail charcoal briquettes. We made our own. We used certain pieces of drift wood, fallen trees and branches that were collected from beach and the vast timberland on the island. The major problem was how to get the wood from the upper levels to sea level. The solution was to methodically tumble the wood in a well-organized plan. Flip by flip over and over again was the method for smaller trees and branches. For the bigger, heavier trees, a rope tied tree was slowly tug/ lugged from discovery spot to beach or near beach location. We then selected prime pieces for "our" charcoal stash. The practice was eventually dropped due to excess time involvement and much hard work. Luckily, we found a place outside of Bar Harbor that made and sold homemade stick charcoal at a fair price.

On special occasions we prepped for a traditional New England Clam Bake. Passed on to early settlers this Native American practice found its way up and down the Atlantic Coast. Slight variations in different places were evident along the eastern coast but the basic stacking pattern and food components were consistent and readily identifiable: a pit in the sand, approximately three feet deep by thirty-six to forty-inch diameter. Stones were heated in a separate fire pit then placed in the bottom of the herb and sea weed covered steam pit. Food that took long to be done were placed on the bottom, followed by food taking less time and so on. A typical bake at a beach would have potatoes, corn, clams, shell fish, like crab, shrimp, lobster or all three when and where available. These were topped with freshly harvested clams. Water was fed slowly to the pit which created steam to cook the pit food. It was quite the feast. We did it to celebrate birthdays and other significant days.

On The Water

One late summer afternoon while on a solo sail venture as the sun was tucked away, an easy, soft breeze came over the waters. Everything stopped which brought calm. It was that special moment which captures our fullest attention and envelops us; a time when consciousness defies limits. This conscious gaze pierces veils, expands knowledge and opens minds to new and highly attractive experiences. Experiences not clarified or conveyed by words. Words are signs for ideas and awareness. This particular experience was delivered by an intuitive knowing. Within the silence, peace and tranquility settled on me. I was connected to other minds. This clairvoyant state provided me with a sense of equality and belonging. Perhaps silence is the equalizer that serves as the language of the universe. This unique sense of kinship, a close connection and certain similarity with all brought unequivocal fondness of and for the unknown, beautifully mysterious mindfulness.

I believe the no wind, calm waters, and absolute silent stillness elicited an inner awareness of my being a child of the universe. No horizon, stratosphere, thermosphere or exosphere divided the whole. It was one, complete harmonious belonging. One total, without parts. The experience was a seamless fabric of awe-inspiring beauty, when a thought pierced the moment. I recognized that the Quicksilver was not moving forward. Sails were flapping and the rudder was slowly floundering about. I did not choose to leave this rare setting of keen insight. To motor out would be sailor heresy and inner being denial. Sails were dropped, boundaries placed on the rudder, anchor activated to avoid an all-out drift. "All is well" I declared as the deck became my rest spot to gaze the vista of stars and vastness of space. "No sleeping in the cabin tonight! I relish in nature's best canopy," I heard myself say.

The winds picked up at dawn and called the ocean to work. Choppy waters knocked against the Quicksilver. The loud thuds awakened me. Following a quick stretch, main sail and jib were raised and readied for some unknown number of nautical miles ahead. As the sun in hasty assent paid attention to its task the QS slid through the water as if it were young and energetic again, though there were occasional screeches and joint groans as it rolled and yawed at times. The QS was a sturdy, well-built craft that was 12-15 years old and showed some wear-and-tearness. I loved the simplicity of this 26-foot vessel of the sea. Made by Pearson Triton, the QS had a fiberglass finish, slept 4 and was very affordable. When I found her, the price was well within my reach. The bumps, dents and patch work kept her value a bit lower than true market value. It was a terrific find. I learned to handle her with confidence and kept an eye on her idiosyncrasies.

"All hands on deck!"

But then, Nancy was not on board today. I turned the boat and headed west. A timely gust set us on our way. We were homeward bound.

Nancy chose to go to Bar Harbor to pick up some supplies. Drinking water did not last long in summer heat. So it topped our list. Her list included salt, some canned vegetables and baked bread. Merlot and Tequila rounded out the list. Little did she know at the time that additions were to join the select tally. While in BH she ran into Jim Becker, who was vacationing with his family. Nancy, thrilled to see Jim, meet his wife and children and share updates, invited them to dinner the next day. She correctly anticipated my return sometime today. It was good news. Serendipity at work? As planned, I sailed in past Otter Cliff and its boulder covered beach. What an awesome sight to gaze the 110-foot cliff, as well, the craft swept by Thunder Hole, an equally enjoyable sight at any time of day. After the QS was tethered in the Bay. I hopped a ride to our cottage via a friend who happened to be passing by on Park Loop Ocean Drive, Route #3 and made my way down to the Beach. I spotted the Saab and knew Nancy was home. From road to beach was normally a 10-15 minute walk but the days beauty caused me to pause, sit and watch the magnificent beauty of the Atlantic waters glistening under the sun. After a few minutes I finished the descent to the beach.

Nancy was quick to share about her meeting Jim and family. The news was stimulating. Jim and I remained in loose contact. Several letters were exchanged updating the unfolding of our lives. We didn't see each other since I disengaged from the "institution" as I called it. Jim was a successful therapist in NYC. He considered pulling the plug in NYC but with two children in their early teens he decided to milk his lucrative situation a bit more. And so he did. Turns out that he married an Anthropologist as well. This was while both were working in Washington, D.C. in the early 80's. Jim was a good friend who remained at my side through all of my post-divorce adjustments. The reunion would be enjoyable.

As per Nancy's instruction, our guests arrived without any serious problems. However, Jim and I needed to relocate his car. The entire task was done within 45 minutes.

"So, Jim, happy you and Nancy bumped into each other. Can you stay with us for a few days?" His facial features told the story as he spoke:

"Well, actually, we planned on being in Portland tomorrow evening. Set schedule, you know how it goes."

"Would love to get you and the family into our sailboat and give you a different perspective of the island. It would be a special occasion with fun and excitement. Nancy could pack a lunch. We could do-in a bottle of Merlot for old-times-sake. The boat is safe and I am a decent navigator of these waters."

"Sounds like something my kids would enjoy. I'm good. Let me run it by Janice. She is an adventurer at heart."

"Good. Be careful walking down this terrain. It gets slippery this time of day."

As the cottage door opened it was obvious that Nancy and Janice wasted no time in getting to know each other while the kids explored the rocky beach.

Nancy spoke first, "That was quick, we thought you would be a while…"

I mirrored in echo-like fashion: "Jim and I always get the job done quickly." Janice nodded, as she entered the banter, "I could tell you a few stories about task completion."

"Let's save that one for our next get together."

"Got something to hide Jim?" She vocalized this with eyes sparkling in a childlike tease.

"You Anthropologists never change."

"Too much digging in the sand!" I was quick to add.

And that pretty much was the way the rest of the night unfolded. As dusk came upon us, we finished dinner and opened another bottle of Merlot. The children left the world of adults and asked about a beach fire. All were in agreement. "Let's gather some wood," I nonchalantly asserted. The fire took the chill out of the evening air. Janice and Nancy rummaged through new stuff in the Anthropological realm. Jim and I caught up a bit on how we were doing. The kids gradually lost the NYC voice and were melting into the magic of Mt Desert Island. It was a good evening which extended well into the wee hours. I showed the kids how the telescope operates and once sure they would do it no harm, set them on their own. Regular "oohs" and "aahs" were evident. After coffee and hot chocolate ran their course, a decision to spend the night on the beach was made to the boys' delight. Sleeping bags and other blankets did the job. A good fire was stacked for the remaining hours. Sleep came quickly upon each of us. The boys were first to rise and gleefully bantered the "old ones" to join them for this special day. Sailing was on their minds. The adult world reluctantly confirmed to the request. Coffee juice, fresh pastry, thanks to Nancy's quick thinking after meeting and inviting the family to the cottage. Cereal kept the boys involved. Then, it was to the sea.

It was another beautiful day on the Island. Clear skies, fair winds and an inviting Atlantic call us to the open sea. We rode in Jim's late model station wagon. Upon boarding the QS, some basic "must-do's" were discussed, life jackets secured, and a quick tour of the crafts capabilities completed, we hoisted sails and were off. We headed east then veered north to see some of the sights. By this time, I was certain that seasickness would not be a problem. Since this was their first sailing experience, I decided to go slow so they would enjoy the total experience of wind, sea and various pitch, roll and yawn. There would be time to open-her-up later on the way back in. They seemed to love it.

"Cool!" "Really cool!" "Let's buy a boat Dad!" "Look at the size of that wave."

"I am glad you like the experience."

"Boy! Wait until our friends hear about this part of the vacation. Mom, please take lots of photos."

We ventured out about two miles, did some fishing, ate lunch and simply enjoyed each other's company.

"It is so good to spend time with you Matt. Wasn't sure I would ever see you again. I knew you were up in this part of the country but knew of no way to make contact. And little did I know that you and Nancy were together again. What a pleasant surprise to find both of you. It's been a great reconnect."

"I fully agree, perhaps we could do it again next summer."

Nancy and Janice nodded in agreement.

"Okay then, lets head in before we lose the late afternoon winds."

The QS pointed west as sails were pulled tight to secure a good firm ride to shore. Upon entering the bay area, sails were dropped and secured. The outboard motor churned us into port.

The ride back to the cottage was slow and parade like. All of us were tired and ready to call it a day.

"Quite an adventure!"

"Well, we wanted you and the family to get the true taste of salt air." Everyone laughed as we neared our home.

"We will drop you off and head back to our hotel, get some sleep and be off in early morning. Thank you. It's been enjoyable." Janice with tear in eye hugged Nancy and me, as did the boys. "Thumbs up time!"

"Glad to help it happen."

The boys came down to the beach with us to gather some gear and then they were off.

Nancy and I were exhausted. We sat outside briefly, ate some leftover soup, had a cup of coffee then went to bed.

And So It Goes

An Indian Summer accompanied by lazy afternoons and pleasant evenings extended the mild and mellow end of September. Time on the water was enjoyable but we devoted most of our time to harvesting the goods from our mini garden. Tomatoes were plentiful thanks to the sandy soil. Peppers were small but tasty. Pole beans climbed to the sky and the lettuce was abundant. The carrots were beautiful as were the two sunflowers which yielded ample amount of seeds. The farmer in us became apparent as we released potatoes from their underground home. Garlic picked and dried back in July was readied for mid October planting. While discussing plans for next spring planting Nancy said "It's amazing how good the forest compost works." We preserved some tomatoes and the corn and squash from the farmers market.

We would soon dry dock the QS for winter. However, minor repairs were done prior to that move. So, at this point we were in fair shape. Our food closet stacked to its capacity underwent a double check. Wood supply checked out okay. Plus, the Atlantic would kick up more as its thunderous waves redecorated our beach. Nancy and Jacob convinced me to encase our garden area. I built a slanted roof to ward off heavy rain and rogue waves intent on destruction. Its construction took time, but the effort proved worthwhile.

It took place then, in the midst of winter prep. It was early on Sunday morning when a firm, but non-intrusive knock awakened us. To our complete amazement, a tall, slender long black, wavy-haired woman stood. Yes, it was Jennifer. "I heard you lived on the Island and decided to see for myself how the man was doing. An overnight train brought me north to Boston." "Well…" was the only word that reached my throat as my flabbergasted mind continued to perplex, knowing that she and Nancy were scanning each other. They knew of each other but had not previously met. A general sense of surrealism prevailed in the elongated moment. There I stood between the rocks of the beach and the ingrained memories of time spent with Jennifer. What a predicament! Profound pleasant feelings flooded my mind laced with numerous questions: Why now?

Why, why so long the wait? Where did she come from? What did she leave? Nancy broke the uncomfortable silence and introduced herself.

"Good to meet you as well. Had no idea you were here with Matt. There is no phone listing, you know. So sorry to intrude."

"Not a problem. Come on in. I'll make some coffee."

The exchange was amicable and most helpful for me. I'm sure Jen had a slightly different agenda.

The sizzle and magnetic pull returned and was difficult to deal with. The chemistry had been on hold all these years. The intense eye contact became more and more pronounced. Nancy did not fail to notice, nor say anything combative. She did, on occasion voice a "well then," or "let's see now," then relocate to another spot in the room. None of us wanted to raise the issue of what was going on here. The atmosphere became intense at times, but at no time was it near boil-point-range. As a matter of fact, it was less and less cumbersome as the three of us appeared to be at ease in such situations. It was fairly clear that the three of us liked each other and there were subtle indications that such an attitude accepted the current situation. The cottage was small with one bedroom and a fair-sized general area. The small leather couch would be a perfect fit for Jennifer.

When the coffee and toast were ready, we sat and caught up on Jen's life.

"I've been back to India twice since I last saw you Matt. Both of my parents passed away last year while I was overseas doing research in parapsychology thanks to a USA educational grant. I thoroughly enjoyed London but came down with pneumonia. The overall experience was taxing and left me with limited energy and a decreased drive. It caused me to wonder about the life I was leading since we parted. She chuckled a bit while saying this in the presence of Nancy. The psychologist, she continued to be open, honest and sometimes very blunt. The all-work, limited-play style caught up with me, some…"

"How did all of this lead you to Maine? Florida is a bit down the road," I interrupted.

"I resigned my post as a professor of Clinical Psych at Florida State last summer, moved to D.C. looking for work in the private sector. Upon seeing first-hand the state of affairs in D.C., I made a decision to bolt the life of a shrink. I had enough money to carry me, plus a healthy 401K. I began to trace my footsteps and search for a new life. Canada was my first choice. Quebec's open venues called to me. However, while driving north in New Hampshire through the White Mountains an awareness of a different location became compelling—it was more a desire or longing to be near the sea, so I went east and into Maine. A cabin rented in Baxter State Park gave me time to think things through. It also gradually eased me into a slower, more natural life pace. By the end of three weeks I was convinced to disconnect from past patterns and begin anew. As we say, all that ends creates a new beginning. Change is good!"

"What amazing similarities each of our three lives share here. We were professional people looking for a way out of the heavily rational, absolutely intellectual, western dominated life style of America in general. Here's to #3 Matt!"

We toasted the commonness, raising coffee cups and laughed aloud at the clunk of clay mugs filled the cottage. Something was driving us to an unknown end or purpose.

"Good bye to academics!" I bantered. "Not only does the ocean constantly reshape the coastline here by removing material from one location to a different point, it appears to be playing a major role in fashioning our destiny. A transition is underway here."

Nancy and Jennifer listened and reflected on the point.

"Let's give some credit to personal desire and choice. There is such a thing called self-preservation you will recall. Look at the way Acadia attracts large numbers to live at and visit this Rock-Sea-Scape."

"I agree," was Jennifer's immediate response.

Jen continued her story: "It was while driving near Bangor that I remembered you were at Acadia. I swung south on alt. Route 1 to

Frenchman's Bay but wasn't quite sure what to do next to find you. It was daunting since no phone or e-mail list existed. I began to ask people questions. By chance I met an older man who remembered you. He said he gave you some advice about staying as far east on MDI to avoid the maddening crowd. That was an outstanding help. I knew you wanted no part of the hustle bustle world, so my search was greatly reduced.

I stayed in Bar Harbor and worked the lower southeastern areas. A few people recognized your name but had no clue to your whereabouts. One lady who sold you a sail patch suggested I check out Jacob Nash in Otter's Cove. She knew him from prior dealings, and he was with you when the sail patch was purchased. I found his place but he was not there. A neighbor said he was out to sea and suggested I might try his friend Matt over in Seal Harbor area. After several days canvassing the area—boy! There's a lot of rock on this island—I heard you were down at the tip of Crowninshield Point. And that is that! I just wanted to talk with you Matt."

"What amazing will power. You really needed to see me." I responded.

Every cell in my body thrust me toward her, wanting to merge with her as always. I needed to be alone with her.

"Nancy could you excuse us?"

Jen and I went outside and climbed the hill behind the cottage. My heart raced to warp speed range, emotions flared, and my brain boggled. I was caught in the teeth of the inevitable without a choice. Should-nots and have-to's aside, it was happening. Once safely away from the beach we stopped, stepped closer to each other and chemical magic flowed as it had its way. We clung to each other in lover's embrace. We entered that timeless enduring sense of now. I was releasing self more and more to the spell. I was also deeply torn and confused.

"Jen, I can't do this! Not now! Let's talk." My face betrayed the declaration.

"You talk! Always talk! Talk! Talk! Talk! I need you to hold me, tell me you still love me. Please Matt, ask me to stay awhile. Please!"

Her body spoke more loudly than her words. Her eyes glistened in plea mode. She was in no way desperate. Jen was Jen, strong, independent and purposeful.

"I miss you Matt. I've never stopped loving you and knew we would reunite someday. I know we can reconnect and create that seamless garment again. Give it a try for our sake."

The last thing I remember is that it was raining. I was upset, highly emotional and perplexed. I know I slipped, and the lights went out.

BOOMERANG

Three weeks later I opened my eyes as a hospital staff member told me I just awakened from a coma. Not only did I suffer a severe concussion, a coma followed immediately.

"Where am I? Am I okay? What happened?" blurted from my lips.

"You're in MDI Hospital. Yes, you are recovering nicely. You gave us quite the scare when they brought you in. What a chore our emergency team had to get you up and out of Crowninshield Point. You were helpless. Thank goodness your two female friends helped get you up the hill. Both women visited daily. At times they came together, at other times they came alone. Each read poems to you, whispered into your ear and hugged and kissed you tenderly." The attending nurse was young, seasoned and very pleasant. It helped to have her usher me back into the world of consciousness.

"Thank your lucky stars Mr. Lubin. You were, at times in water way above your head, but your vital signs rallied every time your life pulse threatened to rob you of your ability to respond to stimuli. Your body accepted nourishment and responded favorably to medical therapy and appropriate tranquilization. You dodged some mild seizures. You are the classic example of how a well-conditioned body aids recuperation in trauma situations. Welcome back!"

She smiled warmly and informed me that the doctors were on their way to see me.

The doctor arrived in a few minutes and introduced himself. "You ducked a bullet. On the ambulance ride from Seals Cove you went into cardiac arrest. The EMS people revived you and got you here shortly after that. Your blood pressure hit the roof. You were heavily stressed and struggled with emotional trauma overload. You're a luck- filled guy. You might have bit the dust. In recent days you've been displaying encouraging signs of coming out of the coma. Restlessness with vocal murmuring, some crying and an indiscernible but repetitive and elongated, what sounded like 'Aye' or 'why…' I am happy to tell you that you are on the mend. A good fight Matt."

After a general check of the usual points, pupil dilation, balance, pulse, heart and an EKG/EEG, the physician stated: "You will be with us for a period of observation and start rehab for a week or so. We'll get some light food into you. Get some rest. See you later, Lucky."

My immediate thoughts went directly to the QS. As well, if it was the third week of October, my garlic needed to be planted. Upon that note, I fell asleep as if I hadn't slept for months and months. Two days later I was told that my sleep set a new hospital record for longest sleep without medicine assist. "Bravo Matt," I muttered to myself as I began to wonder and asked about Jen and Nancy. "They will be allowed to visit tomorrow afternoon" came the answer from my nurse.

The next day at precisely 2:00 p.m. the visitor bell rang true and clear. I heard the sound of familiar footwear approaching the room. I was also certain that one sound was definitely, unmistakably, Jennifer's shoe as she danced upon the tile. Turns out both Nancy and Jen came together. The reunion was heartfelt and without drama. I relished the reunion, tired quickly and rested after a thirty-minute visit. Energy drained, I retreated to sleep and awaited another visit tomorrow.

The same clicking of familiar heels accompanied the 2:00 visitor bell. The pace appeared more relaxed, casual and ordinary today. Both women greeted me sweetly and openly with warm kisses and tender touch. It was so good to see them again as they slowly glued together for me what happened.

"When you turned, fell and struck your head a harsh bruise appeared just above your right eye then up into the forehead. I couldn't revive you. After contacting emergency medical help, thanks to a person parked on the road above us, I ran down to the cottage to get Nancy to help. We brought heavy blankets and covered you with a rain poncho. We kept our heads and reassured each other that you would be okay. The ambulance arrived within 35 minutes. Nancy used first aid techniques to keep your blood circulation up and running and constantly checked your pulse and body temperature. It was a scary time! We helped get you up to the ambulance."

Jen paused, then said with great emphasis: "Your legs seemed to give out and you slipped. You went down hard and struck your head on a fallen branch. It was terrible Matt! So pleased to know you are going to be okay!"

Nancy briefly updated the activities of the last few weeks. "The cottage was secured, and we took a room in the hotel down the street. The doctor said we should visit every day, so the temporary move was necessary for us to do our part in your recovery. All is well at the cottage. The QS is safe and secure. Jacob will continue to check on both while you recuperate. He's going to visit you tomorrow. He is so concerned about you Matt." She smiled knowingly of my confusion, clouded mind and bland stare.

"As Jennifer said, the whole thing was unreal and very trying. Keep up the good work Matt. There is more to tell you tomorrow. I understand you start a physical-therapy program tomorrow. Good luck with your first steps."

Once again fatigue overtook me, the girls left, and I returned to the world of dreams. I felt stronger and was confident that all was well.

Jacob arrived shortly after the girls came the next day. Yes, the familiar clickity clack of Jen's shoes announced their arrival. Jacob tossed his hat onto the bed as he entered the room. "Hey you 'old salt', you getting close to taking a sail." He chuckled and did his best to hold back his feelings. "So good to know you are okay Matt. Sure missed you. All is well with the QS and the cottage."

"Thanks, 'Old Timer.' It's good to see you also. I will be up and running the water real soon.

Stand by, everyone!"

The visit was enjoyable but ended 15 minutes later. Mother fatigue had her way again.

Suffer the impatient.

The first day of therapy was challenging. I hadn't left the room (in conscious state) since I entered. A wheel chair provided some relief, but only within the room. Today was different. The nurse piloted us down the hall to a fairly large, opened-spaced room with many windows which offered natural light.

"What a pleasant change from the four walls of my enclosure. After a brief but thorough warm up massage, a harness was lowered from above and placed on me. Upon instruction, "relax as you are gradually hoisted from the chair which will allow your legs to dangle. We will support you Dr. Lubin." I smiled as the two therapists guided me into the therapy exercise. My hips felt like they were being stretched beyond normal range, but my legs were free-float-like.

"Let us know if you have any pain."

"So far so good."

My sense of feeling was not damaged. I was greatly encouraged by this and began to feel less apprehensive about my condition.

"Enough for today. You did well Dr. Lubin. We will build on your strengths and cater to your weak areas tomorrow. Enjoy the rest of your day."

"That's fine with me. Bye."

Following the fifteen-minute free dangle, I was refreshed by a restful dip into a warm water whirlpool for ten more minutes. I was towel dried, placed in the wheelchair and escorted to my four-wall abode. Lunch followed, which was followed by the sound of the 2:00 p.m. visitor bell and footsteps in the hall.

I was happy to see the girls and enjoyed telling them the highlights of the initial therapy session.

Rehab was slow, painful and at times tedious. Gradual awareness urged me on as did the ongoing support from Nancy, Jen and Jacob. The most frustrating aspect was the continued presence of fuzziness in thinking, delays in speech and balance problem. During the rehab process doctors learned that the concussion was more serious than originally thought. Indicators of deeper damage surfaced and unfolded. Memory loss, delayed cognition and vertigo intensified. My balance was impaired as well. The girls were first to notice the dynamic duo which prompted them to seek consultation with the physicians. Further testing by the Eastern Maine Medical Center in Bangor were not good. A tumor was found in the frontal lobe area of my brain. This deeply entrenched tumor developed next to the parietal lobe. It was further identified as glioblastoma multiform astrocytoma. It's a fast-growing, aggressive type of central nervous system tumor that forms on the supportive tissue of the brain. It causes staggering outcomes like muscle weakness, speech problems, memory loss and decreased ability to think and learn.

Quite a package!

An inner calmness in me persuaded my brain to remain in control and not allow panic to prevail. The doctors present answered the questions catapulting from my lips.

"Can it be cured? Will it kill me? What will my life be like?"

"Well, you will need constant care since falling is a huge problem with this disease, so is walking. Vertigo becomes a semi constant companion. You will need a cane to move around and you will find cognitive functions failing you."

"What treatment options are available?

"A craniotomy can remove tumor tissue to relieve pressure in the brain caused by the tumor. This is a first stage treatment. There is no magic bullet here! The procedure typically can be redone. Radiation and chemotherapy tend to be more effective in retarding the cancer growth."

A profound sobering sense overcame me as I recalled the personal belief that the world knocks us down, fractures us and gnaws at us. The challenge is to embrace the life that remains, continues to encourage us to rise up, and choose to continue on with our life's journey and heal.

"Okay. I need to process this traumatic turn in my life. My rehab is nearly complete. When can I go home?"

"You will be here for a few more weeks depending upon treatment selection. After that, periodic check-ups will be scheduled for you. You would do well to find a place closer to the hospital and away from the shore."

As the doctor's last words trickled from his mouth my mind puzzled at tragic glimpses of no cottage, no more QS on the Atlantic. No more telescope nights. My heart felt the pangs of sharp pain as tears overwhelmed my calmness. At that point Jen and Nancy, who had been briefed of the diagnosis were allowed into the room. A deep, silent hug bathed in tears followed as the two women empathized and shared my loss. I was never so vulnerable. I felt like I was falling into a deep cavern and rescued by friendly arms. Their caring bolstered my droplet of courage and regained a semblance of composure.

"I will make it!" I sobbed. "I'll be okay!"

"We will make it," came the girls echo. "Let's get you back to your room."

The remaining time at the Eastern Medical was pleasant but sad as I slowly overcame denial and embraced my situation. I decided to not take the hospital's recommended treatment plan.

"I will live the remaining days of my life with the help of tranquilizers and pain control meds."

The doctor's roared their disapproval and laid out the obvious consequences, accelerated growth of the tumor and spread of cancer. By not removing the tumor increased pain, dizziness, clouded cognitive functions and a decreased quality of life would gradually occur.

—"So be it! I have the support of two beautiful women who truly love me for who and what I am. What more could I possibly desire beyond that?"

I signed the necessary waivers and left the hospital in early spring. Snow was still on the ground in spots. I found it refreshing to breathe the crisp air as it anticipated and paved way for Spring's parade of green bounty.

We continued to weave our three lives together in creative fashion. Prior to discharge, we further melded our lives by merging life insurance policies, 401K's and other financial resources. Each of us were the other's beneficiary. It secured our future as it would unfold for us. We were on our way again. A few weeks back, the girls orchestrated decisions to abandon the cottage at Crowninshield Point, sell the QS and the telescope. They located and rented a small but cozy one-story apartment on the northwest side of Bangor. I was eager to see it as Nancy piloted the trusty Saab through the winding road several miles from the apartment. As I sat in the front seat the blue sky captivated my eyes, tethered my attention and promised good things ahead. I was happy to be out again, and free to do, within certain limits, whatever I chose. My euphoria was shattered by Jen's shout from the back seat as we entered a sharp turn, "Look out ! "

A truck swerved, crossed into our lane and rammed us head-on.

I was the first to be removed from the wreckage. It looked like Nancy and Jennifer's bloody bodies were trapped in the mangled Saab. The emergency room doctor told me the drunk driver's negligence took the lives of Nancy and Jennifer. "They died several minutes apart as the ambulance was nearing the hospital."

On a chilly day several weeks later, Jacob and I put together a simple ceremony celebrating Nancy and Jen's life. We drank a tequila toast to the joy they brought to life. I carried their ashes to the nursing home where I was living. Jacob promised me to blend, at the proper time, my ashes with theirs and return them to the waters of the Atlantic.

Time passed slowly in grief as I struggled with denial, anger, and depression. During lucid moments I reflected on my life and experiences. Vivid memories laced with inner sorrow on my multifaceted loss dominated my mind. I believe my journey led (took by hand) me to places and situations I needed to be as specific times and locations with select individuals. As my eyes grow old and my body loses ground each day, I am thankful for and embrace my entire life. Dreams were achieved, love experienced, while other dreams were stomped on with hopes shattered by the ongoing involvement with the reality of how fragile our existence on the planet truly is. Actually, my sadness is not about me directly. It is more about: "Why do we die?" "Why do we suffer?" All my studies, reflection and discussions never satisfactorily unraveled these questions.

Nevertheless, I am conscious and continue to live as best I can with the harmony and balance I experience, as fragmented as my life is at times. There are no regrets, but I am apologetic for misdeeds and harm I caused others. I've traveled long roads with distant miles and many smiles. I am who I am and was meant to be. My life comes full circle like the underground river, hidden to common eye, that joins the rain cloud which feeds the lake, flows to the creek, becomes the river, then back to the sea. It is like the grass that follows the sun and finds purpose and fulfillment in the hidden water. I became a minimalist. This allowed me to do choice things by living with less stuff. Personal growth, nature's beauty and the wonders of outdoor natural-style living took on higher value. I sculpted my life as this island demanded. It called me to disconnect luxury and embrace a simpler way. Going cold turkey was no easy task. Basic luxuries did not fall without a battle, they pushed and tugged me to return to what was given up and still craved. The rhythm of the Atlantic, howl of the wind and sea scented air were my unyielding allies in this struggle. We triumphed.

It is a most beautiful day. A day when I could join the grass and water.

It is a good day to die as Native Americans proclaim. If today is that day, I say yes. The time has come. Bring on the hidden waters.

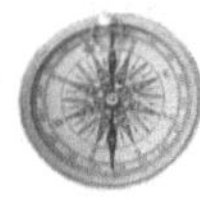

ABOUT THE AUTHOR

Jack with his wife, Donna, and five of
their six grandchildren at the beach.

Jack Esposito has been an educator his entire adult life. He taught two years in a Connecticut high school, and thirty-five years beginning at Niagara University and later as a member of the Adjunct Faculty at King's College in Pennsylvania. He has functioned as a professional change agent training business corporations in team building and employee involvement. He currently resides in Hazleton, PA with his wife Donna.

The couple of forty-four years, raised three children and are continuously taught by six grandchildren. Jack is an avid nature enthusiast, loves to hike and travel. He has written and published poetry since his early days. He enjoys a broad range of music and many friends to match.

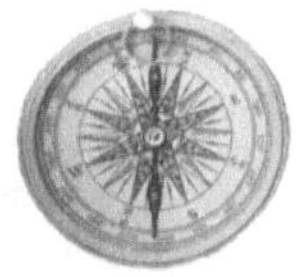